PLAY THE HAND YOU'RE DEALT:

A Crime & Mystery Short Story Collection
Seventeen tales from the mind of
Claire A Murray

O'Cunegan Press, Phoenix, Arizona

I0554462

Table of Contents

Spirit in the Sky...1

Lucky Seven 19

The Drop 21

The Backpack..25

May's Diner 31

Miss Aggie's Pigs 41

After the Rush Fades...47

A Grave Development..59

Danger on the Black Double Diamond...67

Cheating Death...89

April Fools...97

Onta, Tell Me A Story 107

Nanoni and shish-Ka-toomi 109

Most Likely to Succeed 115

The Pixie Path Home 133

Chains.. 151

Tinsel... 159

Kobyashi Maru.. 167

Acknowledgements... 183

About the Author.. 185

Dedication

FOR Pat who was always there, no matter what.
I will always miss you

Print Format ISBN: 979-8-9890501-2-3

Cover Designer: Claire A Murray
Interior Design and Formatting: Claire A Murray
O'Cunegan Press

Introduction

EVERYONE—HERO, VILLAIN, or in-between—is the hero of their own story. Each day presents us with decisions, some of which will lead us down a path toward being one of those. Life throws obstacles in our way, and we play the hand we're dealt because what else can we do?

Life's situations do not determine our character, but we demonstrate our character through the choices we make in those situations. Are we a hero … a villain … or something in-between? Is the Joker there for comic relief or to be the trickster?

The stories in this collection include characters who could be your next-door neighbor, a coworker, a relative … each a hero of their own story whether they are good or bad. There are fanciful stories, too, with other-worldly elements we know don't exist … don't we?

Real heroes, real villains, each trying to get through another day when suddenly faced with a choice and a decision. We hope you find that my friends in these stories have made the right decision or, even if they haven't, that justice was served.

Claire

Spirit in the Sky

JERRY RUSHED TO THE hospital, worry etched into his brow as he sped through a third yellow light, raced up the hill, and found a narrow parking spot on the far end of the lot. Breathless from running when he reached the emergency department, he gasped his father's name at the information desk.

"Oh, Mr. Allen is being seen by the doctors right now. I'll let them know you're here and they'll tell you when you can see him."

Jerry paced in the waiting room until a young doctor called his name. She said everything looked fine but wanted to keep his father for several hours of observation.

"Pops ... I mean, my dad, he's really okay?"

"It wasn't a heart attack, if that's what you mean. We think it was anxiety. He won't tell us much. He doesn't seem to like hospitals."

"Last time he was at one was when my mom died. That was thirty years ago."

"I understand, Mr. Allen. Those memories could add to his stress. Seeing you might help. Please keep him calm. Before you go in, do you know of anything upsetting in his life?"

"No. Nothing. Things are just ... normal, far as I know. He's retired. I run his store and it's doing well, so there are no money problems. He's got friends. We have dinner together a few nights a week. Everything has seemed fine for a long time."

"Well, that's a good reason for us to observe him. He was a little dehydrated so we're giving him fluids. Seniors are vulnerable, especially in the summer. We put in a call to his VA doctor but haven't heard back yet. We won't transfer him to the VA hospital unless he needs to stay overnight. We can talk about that later. It's early in the day."

Jerry put on a calm face and followed the doctor into the long room of curtained cubicles on each side. A few were occupied. Nurses and technicians adjusted equipment and wrote on charts, giving the room an air of busyness. The doctor spoke softly as they approached the far end. "We put him down here where it's quietest. You can stay as long as he remains calm."

Pops looked embarrassed when Jerry stepped behind the curtain and sat beside his bed. "They didn't need to call you. It was nuthin', just nerves, I guess. I must have forgotten to take my cholesterol medicine or something this morning."

"It's okay, Pops. They said you'll be fine and out of here in a few hours."

"I thought it was the big one, ya know? That I was gonna see the spirit in the sky and meet Jesus ... that I'd see Ellie again." Tears formed in the older man's eyes, and he wiped them before they could run down his speckled brown face, skin toughened from years of outdoor activity and wrinkled by time.

Jerry talked about the weather, the shop, baseball, anything except the reason Pops was here. Still, Pops seemed cranky and secretive, mangling the edge of the sheet and not meeting Jerry's gaze. No topic got a good response, so Jerry finally stopped talking.

They waited. The test results and clean bill of health eventually came. Pop's VA doctor phoned in a mild anxiety medication and made an appointment to see Pops a few weeks later. Jerry took his dad home in time for dinner, then slept on the couch after Pops went to bed, still muttering that he "didn't need no nursemaid."

T HE NEXT DAY, Pops made an effort to behave as usual. While Jerry cleaned up after breakfast, Pops sat in his easy chair and played his favorite recording. From the opening distorted guitar riff, through the drums and gospel elements, right to the end, Pops sat motionless and listened. "Spirit in the Sky" had lived in his heart through war, his friendship with his Vietnam buddies Tony and Smitty, love and marriage with Ellie, the birth of Jerry, then Ellie's death. For the first time since he had first heard it fifty years ago, the song did not give him the sense of all being right with his world. The sudden change was jarring.

He pulled a folded sheet of paper from his pocket and examined the crude drawing, a map of the layout for an out-of-town mall. Pops moved to his antique roll-top desk, opened the secret drawer, and shoved the map inside. Jerry's footsteps approached. He slid the drawer shut and straightened a pile of bills on top of the desk.

Jerry entered the room. "What're you doing, Pops?"

"Oh, nuthin.'" The older man dropped the bills back on the desk and settled back into his easy chair.

"How much you need to pay those overdue bills?"

"I don' need no handout or no one hovering over me. They told you at the hospital, it was just anxiety. I got these pills to make sure it don't come back." Pops grabbed a book from his reading pile. "I'll pay those bills come next social security check. Was checking' ta make sure I got 'em all in order."

"Okay. I just worry about you. I want you around for a while longer, you know?" Jerry loomed over the old man's shoulder and read the title, "*Dark Canyon*. You really like that Louis L'Amour guy. How many times have you read this one?"

"Four. Five if you count this time. Now lemme read."

Jerry returned to the kitchen, where Pops heard him setting up for dinner. *Jerry will work at the store late. I can call Tony and Smitty, get 'em to come over to talk about that damned map without Jerry overhearing.*

The back door closed with a squeak and a few seconds later, Jerry's car backed into the street. Setting the book down, Pops closed his eyes and let his mind drift into deep reminiscence of the past fifty years.

I T WAS 1969. Pops was home for a family visit after one tour in Vietnam. As a kid, he was obsessed with collecting Topps baseball trading cards. "You'll see, Dad. Some day these'll be valuable." The nickname had followed, but Topps didn't sound quite right, and his friends changed it to Pops.

While home, he rekindled a romance with his high school sweetie Ellie. She'd let her hair go natural. "No more straightening for me," she told him. He especially liked how the afro created a halo around her head.

They went to the drive-in, danced to the latest music, and he tried to forget about war-torn Vietnam and its rice paddies, fish diet, and oppressive, damp heat. After all, he had to go back.

Between good-bye kisses at the airport, Ellie promised to write often and wait for his return. She pressed a package into his hands. "Open it on the plane."

After takeoff, he discovered it was a small player/recorder, several cassettes, and a playlist for each. She'd recorded dozens of songs, including his new favorite, "Spirit in the Sky," which she'd put on several cassettes. They'd listened to it together many times, feeling the beat, hearing the simple words, and understanding that if you live right you shouldn't be afraid to die.

The song captured his confused feelings about his role in 'Nam. His faith in his decision to serve had been shaken during his first tour. News articles, protests and demonstrations, violent dreams of war when safe at home, and being told by hometown friends he was a murderer had jolted him during his leave. He didn't want to abandon his commitment or dishonor those he'd fought alongside. "Spirit in the Sky" helped ground him. He was prepared to die, if that was to be. He was not a sinner. His spirit would lift upward.

Back on the battlefield, sleep was difficult at first. The quiet nights of home were replaced by constant artillery fire. Each barrage would be followed by deafening silence until nature filled the void with chatter from lizards and birds. When they quieted, soldiers expected more artillery. Whether the sounds were real or dreams, Pops wasn't always sure. If there was no barrage, he'd put the cassette player on low and listen to "Spirit" several times before shutting it off and returning to sleep. His tent mates never complained.

War brought Pops together with two unlikely friends, Tony and Smitty. Tony always had his mind set on how to get rich. Smitty was a relentless womanizer. The two were often in trouble. Pops was their grounding wire, keeping their antics at bay, and getting them out of trouble or talking their lieutenant into giving a lesser punishment. It wasn't a surprise Smitty and Tony never rose in rank. Pops made sergeant.

The lieutenant once told him, "You'd rise farther and faster if you weren't so close to those buddies of yours."

Pops' response was, "Someone's gotta look out for them."

His song became their song. Once, after a week of particularly heavy fighting, Tony said, "I don't know as I believe Jesus is my friend, but I know I'm going to heaven when I die 'cause I'm living in hell right here." Thus, they hardened themselves to the constant presence of death and fought with valor, earned medals for bravery, and accepted that they would either live or die. War had brought them together; the looming specter of death cemented their bond.

The three friends survived Vietnam and returned home with minimal physical scars. After attending Pop and Ellie's wedding a year later, Smitty and Tony moved to Pops' town, and he kept an eye on them. Jerry grew up calling Tony and Smitty "uncle." Pops still had his baseball card collection. He opened a second-hand store and made enough of a living over the years to buy a small house and help Jerry pay for his books for business school.

Pops and Smitty often had to bail Tony out after one of his get-rich-quick schemes failed. Sometimes he was just broke and needed money. Other times, he was in jail. Smitty, womanizing more as he grew older, fell hard for a woman with few scruples. She took him for all his money and left him deep in debt. To dig himself out of that hole, he and Tony cooked up a scheme to rob a bank in a nearby town. Smitty asked Pops for a ride to the bank for the following day, saying Tony needed to cosign a loan for Smitty. He omitted the part about it being a robbery and Pops their get-away driver.

Ellie got sick that next morning, and Pops took her to the hospital. Tony and Smitty attempted the robbery and landed in jail, while Pops worried at Ellie's bedside. Jerry arrived a few days after and stayed with Pops. They laid her to rest a month later.

A neighbor told Jerry about some of the misadventures Pops and his friends had gotten into—small things mostly—the neighbors wondered and worried about. Grateful that Pops hadn't been in on the botched bank robbery, Jerry resolved to keep a closer eye on him. He sold his house, left his job, and bought a condo less than a mile from his childhood home to "keep a closer eye on Pops." He told Pops he'd take care of the shop, which was now open only three days a week. "I'll get it back open full time, Pops, wait and see."

Jerry opened every day, even on Saturdays, while Pops stayed with the three-day schedule he'd grown used to. They worked well together despite many years of being apart. The shop was still in Pops' name, but Jerry managed it and handled all the paperwork. His business degree, experience, and what he'd learned growing up in the shop made him a savvy businessman who knew how to assess items, haggle comfortably with customers, and turn a profit. Jerry tucked away some of the profits for the day when Pops could no longer live on his own.

Years passed and Pops retired, leaving the store fully in Jerry's hands. He modernized and expanded it, adding selected antiques. One corner, though, he kept much as it had been during his father's heyday. Posters from the 60s and 70s were behind the cases. Other sale items included vintage radios, jukeboxes, vinyl records, music cassettes and players, buttons, and bumper stickers. In the center display case, not for sale, was Norman Greenbaum's *Spirit in the Sky* single, Pops' trading card collection, and photos of Pops with friends, mostly from his days in Vietnam with Tony and Smitty.

A FTER LEAVING POPS to his book, Jerry saw a neighbor watering flowers in her front yard and stopped to update her on his dad's condition.

"Mrs. Peach, got a minute?" As a child, Jerry had played with her son Peter. She'd called the ambulance yesterday after seeing Pops stagger past her house.

She turned, her brow furrowed, then smiled. "Jerry, how's your father doing? I've been so worried. Was it a heart attack?"

"No, nothing like that. It was anxiety, they think. Say, does he walk by here every day?"

"Oh, yes. Just about every morning and evening. We wave to each other."

"He never told me. In fact, he doesn't tell me much lately. That's why I stopped. I'm worried about him." Mrs. Peach was the neighborhood busybody and would be the first to know if something fishy was going on. "He's getting older. I don't want to hover, but he's my dad ...."

She shut off the water and hung the hose on a hook. "Come inside and I'll fix you a cup of coffee. I made brownies. Would you like one?"

"Sure. That would be nice." Jerry followed her to the kitchen in the back. Through the curtains, he could see the blurry outline of Pops' kitchen. Jerry asked about Peter, and that got Mrs. Peach on a long-winded track he wished he hadn't started. He finally steered the conversation back onto his father. She had little to offer, and he didn't want to say anything that would lead to gossip. She agreed to call him if she heard or saw anything suspicious.

Driving to the store, his thoughts centered on Pops' anxiety attack, why he'd become so cranky lately, and whether his mental faculties were still intact. Jerry knew decline was hard to spot in someone you were close to and saw daily. If his father needed medical or long-term care, would there be enough money? Pops had antiques at home and in the store. Internet research and a talk with Pops' VA doctor were definitely in order.

At the store, he surfed Internet sites for roll-top desks and learned Pops' desk was hand built, which likely dated it to before the 1860s. That could fetch a good sum, even with the wear and tear of life in the Allen home. There wasn't a time Jerry couldn't recall it being there. He'd sat at it to do his homework, played under it with his trucks. Pops' had bought it when he first opened the shop, then kept it for himself. He might not want to part with it, but if the time came, Jerry would sacrifice that desk to make Pops comfortable. He saved his search and closed the browser when a customer came in, then was busy through the rest of the afternoon and into the evening. Jerry called Pops to make sure he'd taken his medication and got a scolding in return, not like Pops at all. He closed up and went home, a worry frown etched into his forehead.

T HAT SAME EVENING, Pops answered the door to let Smitty and Tony in. They sat in the living room and clinked their beer bottles together before Tony asked, "So, you in or not, Pops? We gotta do this soon."

Pops shook his head and said nothing.

"It's foolproof. We can do this," Smitty said. "We did it all the time in 'Nam."

"You got caught a bunch o' times in 'Nam ," Pops said,

Tony said, "Only those times you weren't there. You're our Jesus factor."

"You mean you used me—" Pops said. "Got me all figurin' we was never gonna get caught and if we did, well it was all right anyway. I finally got some sense and stopped. But you two kept right on goin' and I kept rescuin' ya. I was a fool to let you play me, let that song go to my head."

Smitty said, "We're doin' it, with or without you. If just me and Tony do it and get caught, that's on you."

"I don't know. Too risky without Pops. We ain't young like back then," Tony said.

"See, Pops? We need you," Smitty said.

Pops banged his beer bottle down on the coffee table, sending a spray of drops onto the wood. "Go away. I gotta think on this. I been bailin' you two outta trouble for fifty years and you still don't learn." He led them out the door and cleaned up the empties, muttering all the while. "They think Jesus or me is gonna get them outta their scrapes. I swear, I don't know no longer where I'm goin' when I die. I wish Ellie was here. She always set me straight after them two was around."

POPS' CHECKUP AT the VA was normal for a man of his age. Cholesterol was still a little high, heart normal, blood pressure good, and blood tests from the hospital had come in and were fine. There was nothing physically wrong. "Has anything been worrying you, Mr. Allen? Do you get enough sleep? Have enough money to pay your bills? Is anything unusual going on at home?"

"Nuthin's bothering me or like that. I got enough money and Jerry here runs the store good, made it run better over the years. I don't know why I had that attack, if that's what you're getting at. I just want to go home and go about my business."

The doctor said Pops should stay on the anxiety medication a while longer, switch to decaf, and take his blood pressure daily. On the trip home, Jerry said, "Look, Pops, if something's been bothering you. You can, tell me. I love you. I don't want to lose you. Whatever it is, we'll get through it together."

"There's nuthin' to get through, Jerry. I'm fine. Just take me home and go back to the shop. You don't want that college kid running it for too long. He might sell the whole store too cheap."

"He won't. He's a business major and likes working there. We should stop and get dinner. We haven't been out to eat in a while."

"No. I want to go home." Pops stamped his foot on the floorboard. "I got things to do. You go about your business."

Jerry dropped off Pops and returned to the store. During lulls, he pulled up his research on antique desks and learned some had hidden cavities or drawers. He'd never explored Pops' desk, just played beneath it. He did more research and made notes on possible locations.

T HE NEXT MORNING, Pops met Smitty and Tony at a diner on the outskirts of downtown. "Jerry has been dropping in on me sometimes. I need to talk with you two without him around."

"Sure, Pops," they chorused back. The waitress brought water and offered menus. "Coffee, gentlemen?"

Tony and Smitty said yes; Pops asked for unleaded, his name for decaf. They ordered without looking at the menus. When she was out of earshot, Pops faced his two comrades and kept his voice low. "Look. You knuckleheads have gotta cut this out. I ain't always gonna be around to bail you outta trouble."

"What're you saying, Pops? You sick or somethin'? You was at the hospital." Tony looked closely at Pops, who calmly unrolled flatware from his napkin.

Smitty settled back in the booth and pointed at Pops. "Naw, Tony, look at him. He's the picture of health. He's just being cautious, like always."

"I'm bein' smart. This plan of yours ain't gonna work. Things are different today. Too much technology. Too many cameras. There's no Jesus spirit gonna take you to the Spirit if you keep actin' like fools and gettin' inta trouble. And I ain't gonna be there to get you out. I'm done." He sipped at his coffee and rummaged in the condiment bin. "All this non-sugar crap's gonna kill me. Where's the damned sugar?"

The waitress returned with their orders, and the three dug in. Between bites, Tony and Smitty tried to talk Pops into helping them. As the lunch crowd began to filter in, Smitty threw down his napkin and said, "All right, Pops, we get it. You won't help us. Give us back the map."

Pops looked at his friend. "You're gonna go through with it?"

"Hell, yes. It's my lifeline. I got nothing left to lose."

Pops looked at Tony. "And you're gonna help him?"

"You bet. I'm ashamed you won't. Thought you was our friend."

"I am your friend, both of you. I'm tryin' to save you from yourselves."

Smitty said, "Give us the map, Pops. We'll handle this on our own."

"Didn't bring it. Thought I could talk sense into you two. Thought maybe you'd grow up some day, especially after last time. Instead, you come up with this fool plan. Well, whatever happens, I ain't gonna have no part in it and I ain't bailin' you outta jail when you gets caught."

Tony stood and threw money on the table. "Tonight, Pops. We're coming over and you'll give us what's ours. C'mon Smitty. Mr. Right needs his privacy."

Smitty threw a few more bills on the table and left with Tony. Pops sat for several more minutes, tears streaming down his face. The waitress brought the check and more decaf. She said, "You all right, honey? Did those two do something to you?"

"Oh, I'm okay. Just sad. Some folks don't never grow up. Always have to be the fool, ya know?"

She put a hand on Pops' shoulder, "Yeah, I know. See it every day. Look, let me take this. You don't pay for your breakfast. Let me do that for you." She picked up the loose bills and let him compose himself.

Pops left the diner and walked the length of the town common and back. He couldn't give them the map. It was too risky. They'd get caught and at their age, the time they'd spend in jail, well, it would kill them. He sat on a bench, head in his hands with his elbows propped on his knees.

A young man sat down next to him. Pops looked up into a set of green eyes that almost matched the camouflage uniform he wore. Green Eyes said, "You okay, mister? You look kinda sad."

"Yeah. I am."

"Wanna talk about it?"

"You military?"

Green Eyes pointed to the name stitched on his right pocket flap, "Lieutenant Greenbaum, at your service. Two tours in Afghanistan."

"I was a sergeant ... in 'Nam."

"It's an honor, sir."

"Hmph. That's something I never heard when I came back. You still in?"

"Recruitment center," he pointed across the street, "right over there between the diner and pizza shop. You look like a man with a problem. Maybe I can help, sir."

Those green eyes said, *trust me*.

"Call me Pops."

They talked for hours. Pops went home with a light heart and the beginnings of a smile on his face. He had a friend in Jesus after all.

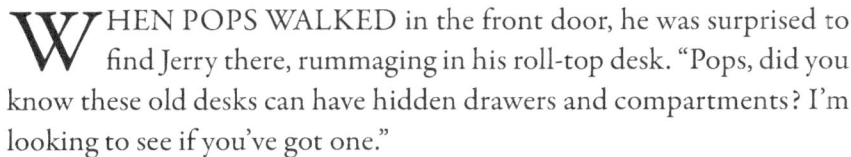

WHEN POPS WALKED in the front door, he was surprised to find Jerry there, rummaging in his roll-top desk. "Pops, did you know these old desks can have hidden drawers and compartments? I'm looking to see if you've got one."

"You leave that alone. That's mine. You can explore it when I'm dead."

"Pops, don't say that. I want you around for a long time. But don't you see? There could be something important, something valuable, in this desk. It could add to your retirement money."

"I said leave that desk alone." Pops shoved Jerry away from the desk.

Jerry stood and stared at his father. "You've never talked to me this way before. What's gotten into you? I only want to help and lately all I get from you is argument and 'leave me alone.' Crap like that. That's not you, Pops. What's wrong?"

Pops shook his head. "I'm sorry, son. I got some things on my mind, that's all. Nuthin' to do with you."

Jerry led Pops to his easy chair and helped him sit. "Tell me what's wrong. Please. Let me help."

"Naw, I got me some help. It's gonna be all right. Now get out of here. Tony and Smitty are comin' over, and I don't want you here."

"Those two. I bet your anxiety has something to do with them. I'm not leaving until I know what it is."

"No. I was worried about them, but I tell you, I got this covered. Now let me be. You'll spoil everything if you stay."

"Pops, you got to tell me. I think maybe you aren't yourself. Something is worrying you fierce. I don't want to see you back in the hospital. I'm not leaving until you spill it all."

Pops relented and told Jerry about the hidden drawer. He retrieved the map, showing the location of alarms at a store with a safe that Tony could crack, and revealed Tony and Smitty's plan.

Jerry was shocked. "You mean they've been doing stuff like this for years? Man, can you keep secrets."

"Now you know why I didn't want to tell you. It'll spoil everything. I don't want them to go to jail, but I can't help them do this."

"So what're you gonna do, Pops, give them the map?"

"Yes."

"That's crazy. They're bound to get caught."

"I know. But I can't help them this time. I told them so today."

Pops swore Jerry to secrecy and ushered him out the door. He sat in his easy chair and waited for his two friends.

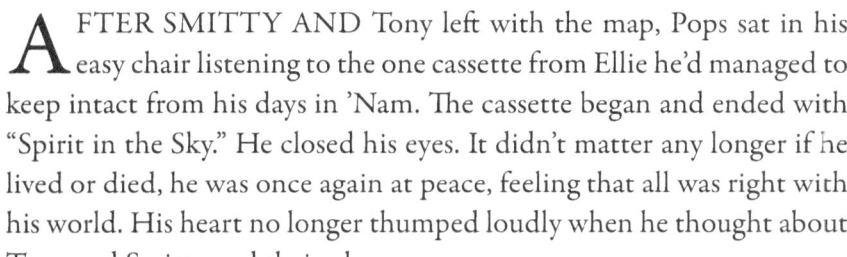

AFTER SMITTY AND Tony left with the map, Pops sat in his easy chair listening to the one cassette from Ellie he'd managed to keep intact from his days in 'Nam. The cassette began and ended with "Spirit in the Sky." He closed his eyes. It didn't matter any longer if he lived or died, he was once again at peace, feeling that all was right with his world. His heart no longer thumped loudly when he thought about Tony and Smitty and their plan.

He wished he could be a fly on the wall where the robbery was to take place. It would certainly be tonight because once those two had their hands on the map they would spring into action, each never quite trusting the other with sole possession. That's why they'd left it in Pops' hands. They'd done similar things over the years, always pulling Pops into their plans even though he wouldn't go with them on their escapades. He was the one point of total trust between them. It had been that way since they'd met.

His phone rang at midnight. After the call, he sat back and smiled, then sighed. He hoped this would be it: the final crazy, stupid, jackass idea from his two buddies. He picked up his car keys and drove to an old warehouse downtown.

"Pops, glad you could make it." Lieutenant Greenbaum, in dark clothing and no military insignia, stepped out of the darkness and shook Pops' hand. "Want to see the interrogation?" At Pops' nod, he led him to a small room with a one-way mirror and they watched as first Tony and then Smitty were interviewed separately. The two clearly thought they'd spend the rest of their days in jail although they couldn't figure out what police station they were in and kept demanding their right to a phone call.

Pops looked at his new friend. "You didn't rough 'em up none, did you?"

"Nope. My buddies treated them right. You won't find a bruise or mark on them. I've stayed out of sight all along, so they'll never know even if they see me on the street."

"That's good. Thank you. What happens next?"

"That's up to you? You want to go in there and talk to them? Separately? Together? Spill it that this part was your setup?"

"Won't do no good. They'll take it as me bailin' 'em out. Had an idea, though, while waitin'."

Lieutenant Greenbaum agreed to Pops' plan and after a short while, Jerry met them in the warehouse. "Jeez, Pops. How'd you manage all this?"

"Not me. Him." Pops pointed to his new friend, then looked at his son. "Now, got your story straight?"

"Yup. You told me about their plan. I listened to a police scanner and learned when they'd been picked up. I talked the police into letting two 'Nam vets go on account they got no brains between them."

"Yeah. That'll work. Just make sure they know the cops are on to them and will be watchin.' If they ever pull anything again, they're toast."

"Got it."

After Jerry met with Smitty and Tony, Lieutenant Greenbaum's buddies blindfolded and led the two out of the warehouse. "For your own protection," they told each man when dropping them off at their homes. "We don't ever want to see your names on any arrest warrants or even see you in our station again."

The next day, a subdued Tony and Smitty had lunch with Pops after he called and said to meet at the diner. The same waitress took their order. She looked closely at Pops, who winked.

Smitty handed the map to Pops. "Burn it, eat it. Just destroy it before it destroys our lives. We decided to pass. Not just on this one. We're done, for good."

"Sounds like you two growed up sudden-like."

"Yeah. You could say that," said Tony. "I'll find another way to pay off my debts."

Pops said, "You could start by takin' some advice 'steada all them schemes you come up with." He slid a piece of paper listing numerous resources across the table. Lieutenant Greenbaum had come up with it right after Pops had met him.

"Yeah. I shoulda' been listening to you all along, Pops. You've always tried to help us, teach us. Guess we never appreciated how smart you are."

"Not smart. Practical. And I listen to smart people."

Smitty said, "Pops, can you forgive us for what we said yesterday? It was mean. I realize, Tony realizes, you was watchin' out for us like always, like we're still a team."

"Yep," said Pops, "that's what it takes, a team." Pops nodded ever so slightly to Lieutenant Greenbaum, watching from the booth behind Tony and Smitty.

Lucky Seven

I WAS NEVER LUCKY. Made one bad decision after another. Then, an unlucky roll of the dice left this Nebraska farm gal stranded in Vegas, owing Nicky Stones a bundle. Last week he warned me to leave Vegas. I didn't listen.

The blackjack tables didn't entice me, although plenty of other dames sidled up to the tuxedoed players. Craps, that's my game. Those tables were hoppin'. I smoothed my gown and hustled over. Watched how the dice were running.

In craps, winning and losing numbers depend on where you are in the game. Roll seven or eleven in phase one—the Come Out roll—Pass bets win; Don't Pass bets lose. Roll seven or eleven in phase two—after Point is set—Pass bets lose; Don't Pass bets win. Sounds confusing, but this gal has a brain for numbers, rules, and betting combinations.

I dug into the pocket of my evening bag. The one chip I'd managed to save slid into my fingers and I set that thousand-dollar orange chip on Pass, praying Nicky's table crew didn't recognize me, hair newly dyed blond, bright red lipstick—no Nebraska here.

"Seven." The stickman pulled the dice back. I'd doubled my money. And my heart rate. I fanned myself and added my win—another orange chip—to my original. Shooter rolled again.

"Four. Point." Phase two began, with the shooter needing to roll another four to win. He won that round, but not the next. I'd bet against him and won. New game. The player to his left became the shooter.

Evening slithered into night. Shooters and players came and went. The bright lights glittering off sequins, lighters, and metal fixtures tricked one's senses with the false aura of daytime. I changed my bets, reading players and dice like never before. Noise and the crowd at the table grew, along with cigarette smoke and my winnings. I grabbed a drink and shut out all but the table. The dice went to the player on my right. I bet against him.

"Three." The crowd groaned at the losing Come Out roll. The shooter glared at me, as if my bet had caused his downfall. He lifted a drink off the tray of a passing hostess, not even ogling the scant outfit over her butt as she walked away.

He stalked off, but I was elated; I had enough to pay off Nicky and go back home. Not that I'd ever leave Vegas. Gambling was legal. Prohibition was over. Vegas was the new Wild West, with few laws and fewer lawmen.

I rolled eleven on the Come Out. Nicky came down from his office. No surprise. I was on a streak. The house was losing. I rolled again

"Six. Point."

All my chips were on Pass. Nicky closed the table to everyone but me. I could feel the crowd suck in its breath.

"Double or nothing, Nebraska?" he asked through tight lips.

I nodded, too stupid with greed and revenge to stop myself. I wouldn't lose. I just knew it.

The stickman slid the dice over. I rolled.

"Seven." The stickman scooped the losing combo back as the crowd groaned.

THE NEON SIGN above the club shone through the backseat window in my final ride to the desert. I'll never leave Vegas.

The Drop

"C'MON. YOU'LL REALLY love it. The view is fantastic."

"I don't know, Doug. It sounds kind of scary. Why do you call it *The Drop*?"

"Oh, it's amazing. You're walking along and there's all sorts of trees and scenery and then ... Boom! You're at a drop-off. Go too fast and you could drop right off the edge."

"It's a long fall to the bottom?"

"Oh, yeah, a long fall."

"You'll warn me, right?"

"Oh, yeah, I'll warn you. Don't worry, honey. The view is worth it."

She let him convince her over dinner, playing doubtful and finally giving in, before he angered. *Why spoil his fun? Maybe it'll be okay and remind him of our first time here, keep him calm.*

She'd picked this camping area for a holiday weekend several years ago. Speaking on impulse, she said she'd read about it in a travel journal. That was her first lie to Doug, because she had come here frequently as a child and been to *The Drop* many times. Had she instinctively known about his true nature?

On that first trip, she kept them close to the cabin. When he began making solo camping trips after that, she suspected he was coming here. Today's knowledge of *The Drop* confirmed her suspicions.

So far, they'd followed the same patterns, doing what Doug wanted, him pouting if he didn't get his way. *I wonder if I should confront him about the affair? Hmmm ...maybe not. This isn't the best place to get medical help if he gets angry. I don't know if he knows I know. Then again, I'm not sure he even cares.*

Their storybook relationship throughout high school and college seemed destined for *happily ever after*, the football star and head cheerleader. Then she became ill and wasn't as physically active as before. He reacted as if the diagnosis was intentional and all in her head. Lately, he flaunted his strength and power, demanding physical activities that were difficult for her even when she had lots of preparation and rest. Rheumatoid arthritis saps your energy even as it destroys your body.

Secretly, she joined a gym with a pool, exercising and swimming to keep her body as strong as it could be. But that would only take her so far. If he knew she could keep up with his hiking, climbing, and other challenges, he'd add more. That was his game—wear her down, then berate her for being weak. The pattern had emerged not long into their marriage, shortly after her diagnosis. The past five years had been a constant physical and emotional struggle. The physical bruises faded, but the emotional ones were constantly refreshed.

THEY SET OUT before dawn, grass wet with dew, birds and squirrels starting their day. The well-marked trail narrowed after several miles, showing fewer signs of travel. They stopped to eat the bacon, biscuits, and hard-boiled eggs she'd packed for breakfast, with hot coffee in a metal thermos she brought.

What is his fascination with The Drop this weekend? Is he planning to get rid of me and say it was an accident? I wouldn't put it past him. He did force me to increase my life insurance policy last year. Has he been planning this all along? How has my life come to this?

"Why'd you have to bring that heavy pot, honey? We could skip the coffee for once."

"Oh, I thought you'd like a hot cup before resuming the hike. I want the weekend to be special. I added cinnamon, just the way you like it."

She smiled and handed him the metal cup. Doug was calm, not gruff or snarling. In fact, he seemed extra considerate of her today. *It's as if he's made a decision.*

He led the way off the main trail to a steep path. The burn in her legs was what she had prepared for at the gym. She lagged behind intentionally, not wanting Doug to know how fit she really was. *If he knows I can keep up, he'll add more difficult challenges tomorrow, when I need to rest.*

They'd spoken little since breakfast, each wrapped in their own thoughts. They'd been alone for hours. From the sun's angle, she figured it was about ten o'clock.

They were nearing *The Drop*.

Pine, maple, ash, and poplar trees blocked much of the sun, making the trail cooler than if they'd hiked the more open trails to the east. She couldn't identify most of the plants but took deliberate steps to stay on the path and preserve the forest's ecosystem. She was munching on a wild apple from the batch they'd picked in the clearing where they'd eaten breakfast. Doug's backpack held more apples. Her pack had the wrappings from breakfast tucked safely inside, with the thermos snugged to the outside.

The trail leveled off before reaching the tree line. *Stay alert. Let him lead.*

"Honey, we're almost there. Watch your step." Doug stepped aside and motioned for her to pass.

"Oh, no, Doug, you lead. I can keep up." She bent forward, panting as if winded. Even though the trail was level, they'd been hiking for hours and her energy levels fluctuated, so this would appear normal.

"If you say so. But I want to see the look on your face when you catch this view." She seen a hint of the open vista as they'd turned with the trail. *Don't let on. It's supposed to be a surprise.*

Doug disappeared around the turn of the path, his back to her, then reached back to pull her forward, as he'd done on the more difficult parts of the climb.

She straightened quickly, snapping the heavy thermos off its catch, and rushed forward. With one swing, the heavy thermos connected with his skull, shock registering on his face.

The Drop was aptly named. His body was hidden from view and she never heard it hit the ground below. The last sound had been his voice, fading away.

"Whyyyyyy?"

"Poor Doug. Don't you remember that when we increased my life insurance, you increased yours? I never trusted you since the first time you hit me, long before I showed you the lovely cabins I said I'd read about. I've waited a long time, but now I get something for my pain and suffering all these years and you, well ... you know what they say in all those westerns you made me suffer through—'I've got the drop on you.'"

The Backpack

I WOKE IN A SWEAT IN the pitch black of a moonless night in Henry's cabin. My ears worked just fine, however. Low, raspy voices chanted my name, sending a chill up my spine and ending at the base of my neck, my hairs bristling like a dog's. I knew Henry had gotten into witchcraft and other stuff I didn't believe in. But suddenly, ice filled my veins, creeping from my fingers to my arms, then my neck. My toes, feet, and legs came next. I couldn't stop shivering. Was that eyes peeking at me through the walls? I shook my head and the vision passed. The voices remained.

Hands shaking, I lit a match, successful after the first four ended up on the floor. The voices receded into the depths of the walls. Match flickered out; the voices resumed. I groaned, got up, and lit the lantern. Ahhh ... silence. Opening the trap door in the floor, I couldn't resist one last taunt. "Henry, you're a real killjoy, little brother."

I sat in the wooden chair by the ramshackle table, head in my hands. Was I sweating or had the ice in my veins turned to water? We shoulda been celebrating. But no, by the time we'd left the sleepy town of Gila in our dust and made it to his cabin in the Sonoran Desert, Henry'd growed a conscience.

He'd never told me why he wanted the money, and I'd never asked, but I could tell it was important to him when he'd laid out the plan on a prison visit. He just needed me for backup. Hey, give me my cut and I'm happy. So I'd said yes.

We'd got to the cabin and counted the money, but Henry was still moaning over me using a loaded gun. No one was supposed to get hurt, he said. Yeah, like ya know, it doesn't always work out that way. But Henry kept on about it.

I'd finally had enough. "So what if I shot that teller? Damned idiot was about to press the alarm button. Then where'd we be?"

"Bad juju, brother. Our Karma's gonna be all messed up," Henry restuffed the money into his backpack. "We gotta give this back, set things right."

"Seems to me you're already messed up. That's what comes from foolin' with that witchy stuff." I tried to take the pack from him, but he clung to it like it was all his.

"Don't say stuff like that." Head hunched into his shoulders, his squinted eyes darted around the cabin. He lowered his voice. "They'll hear, take revenge."

I let go of the pack. "Who'll hear, Henry? What're you talking about?"

"Shssh." He seized a purple bottle off the shelf over the stove and cradled it and the backpack in his arms. "Bad Karma will come back on us. We took a man's life. Gotta do the right thing now."

Hoo boy, was he messed up. I guess I'd missed too many of his growin' up years and he'd imagined friends with these spirit things. Poor kid. Just had me after mom and pop died and I hadn't been around much, exceptin' when I'd needed a driver for a heist. Henry was a good driver. Usually.

I ran my hands through my hair and said, "Don't know what happened to you while I was in prison, but you done gone plain crazy." I snatched the bottle out of his arms.

Henry shouted some weird mumbo jumbo and dropped the backpack. Then he came after me, eyes fixed on the bottle. How could that bottle be more important than the money?

I didn't think a whack off the head would've kilt him like that. But there he was, laying on the floor like a sack o' flour and me standin' there with that heavy purple bottle. Only now it was purply-red.

I got tired of walking around his body in that one-room cabin filled with special candles and masks for his crazy ceremonies, so I dumped him and all of that crap into the crawl space below the floor. Prob'ly made durin' prospectin' days. Good place to hide if you weren't sure whether someone coming across the desert was gonna visit or steal. I can use it if I ever need a hidey-hole after a job. Henry'd said the cabin was paid off, so I guess by rights it belongs to me now.

I went to bed, figurin' I'd hightail it out in the morning and spend a few months south, maybe Mexico. Let the heat of the robbery die down.

Then them voices had started. I wasn't gonna get any sleep now. I sat in the kitchen, lookin' at the trap door, and drunk from the tequila I'd bought in town, hopin' to warm my bones. Them demon voices still had me shiverin'. I must've dozed 'cause I woke up in the chair with a stiff neck and the empty bottle on the floor beside me.

I couldn't leave Henry's body in the crawl space. Wouldn't be right, him bein' kin. It'd be like I'd run away without sayin' goodbye. So I drug his body outside and set it beside a tree. Birds were chirping. Sun was comin' up. I buried him right quick, the rotting tree giving me no trouble about roots. I was finally warm, what with the digging and the sun. I tossed all the mumbo jumbo stuff beside him and put that purply-red bottle in his hands. I didn't want nothin' to do with it, but it was important to Henry.

I covered him up, but you could tell the ground's been dug. I went back into the cabin and grabbed the plants Henry had all over. Mostly different types of cactus and a few bromeliads like the ones Mom used to keep in the house. I never had no use for plants, 'specially in the desert. They just use up water.

I planted them, pots and all, over Henry's grave, hoping no one would notice they don't take up as much space as I'd dug. Maybe. If I was lucky. Don't feel lucky right now.

I searched around and found some large rocks behind the cabin. Carried them over to the grave and set them in the bare spots. It looked better. I drug an old chair from the back and set it between the new garden and tree. Didn't know I had it in me to make somethin' like that.

Clouds were gathering when I finished, a needed break from the sun's heat. I had to hit the road, in case anyone's checkin' out desert cabins for two bank robbers. I said a few words first. "It's fittin' I'm leaving you here, Henry. We'd a parted ways pretty soon if you was alive. Your mumbo jumbo don't fit in my life. I sure don't fit in yours."

I grabbed his backpack. Along with the bank money, it held a baloney-and-cheese sandwich—his favorite—and a book—*Tales of the Revenged*. Huh. Crazy mumbo jumbo. But it hid the money, so I left it there and closed the pack. That's when I seen it. HENRY—stitched in bright colors on the outside flap. Hadn't seen that when we was in the bank and prayed no one else had either. Hoisting it onto my shoulder, I left Henry's car behind and walked south into a thunderstorm.

Henry'd always been following me around growin' up. Mom would've whupped me good for leavin' him behind, so I'd learned him how to drive and be my getaway guy. It'd worked out okay 'ceptin' for that last time. I should've offed him for takin' off in the car and leavin' me behind in the bank just 'cause a cop had driven by. Come to think of it, he'd just been gettin' into mumbo jumbo back then.

My footsteps, crashing thunder, and pelting rain were the only sounds as I walked for miles. The rain felt good, like it was washing my skin and sins clean. Maybe I am lucky.

Mexico here I come. I kept to the edge of the road so's to hide behind them big cactus if I heard a car. None came.

Soggy and downtrodden, even after the storm rolled out, I camped a ways off the road, with only Henry's sandwich for dinner. I'd take a cold steak and cheese sub any day over baloney, but Henry had his ways. Every day he'd eat the same thing. I'd take him out for lunch and, like a little kid, he'd ask for baloney and cheese. Momma had said he was special, whatever that means.

I bed down under the stars with the backpack as a pillow, cursing Henry. I'd spent eight years in the pen to protect him, while he bought into crazy witchcraft and Karma and that garbage. I'd 'a got out in four if I'd given up his name. Instead'a bein' grateful, he wanted to return the loot. Never should have listened to him. His sudden conscience made it go bad. Worse for Henry, though. Life was funny like that.

"Well, Henry, looks like your Karma got run down or just plain up and left you." I rolled onto my side, the hard earth digging into my hip. At least I had the money.

Voices woke me. Different from the raspy demons in Henry's cabin, these were loud, clear, and accompanied by the *chuck-chak* of a rifle bein' cocked. I opened one eye and wished I hadn't, seeing as the barrel of a shotgun was pointed in my face. No, these weren't the mumbo jumbo voices from the cabin. Them spirits wouldn't be arresting me for robbery and Henry's murder.

I fessed up, hours and many cups of lukewarm coffee later, after I learnt that lightning had set fire to the tree outside Henry's cabin. By the time the police stopped there, the tree had toppled, and deep roots had upheaved his body. It hadn't taken long for teams searching the road in both directions to find me, with Henry's name stitched on the backpack. I swear his name was glowing and pulsing when they pulled me to my feet, but none of 'em had seemed to notice.

Should've buried it with Henry.

May's Diner

MORNING SUN SHIMMERED across Eagle Lake as it rose above the trees and bounced off the copper pans lining the wall of May's diner. It was a wonder anything could cut through the greasy windowpanes: May wasn't known for cleaning much except her cast iron skillet and copper pans.

A Georgia transplant thirty years ago to this quiet Maine town near the Canadian border, she'd kept her soft southern drawl. Her smile emphasized dimpled cheeks as her figure broadened with years of eating her own cooking. May smiled at everyone, always had a kind word, and folks gravitated to the diner throughout the day. Even the most down and out left smiling.

Squinting against the golden glow cast off the pans, May began breakfast for her first customer of the day. "Morning, Dan."

He grunted and took his customary stool—last seat on the short elbow of the L-shaped counter, next to the back room washup and pantry. Told May once he liked the view, but she figured it was to watch his truck and the diner entrance. Some people are like that, her late husband had once said.

Grits simmered in another pan while the coffeemaker spat the last dregs into its carafe. May served grits with every breakfast, even if the customer didn't order them. She angled the heavy skillet to spread bacon fat over the surface, and with one hand cracked two eggs against the edge, dropping them in with a sizzle, yolks intact. "Going fishin' with Phil?"

"He's gone backwoods alone to fish some stream he favors. I gotta sell that load out there soon's I eat. Maybe sell the truck, too. It got stuck on a ridge in Wallagras last Sundee, bed full of heavy rock. Don't know why I bought that thing from Phil. Always gettin' stuck somewheres. He lent me that hauler outside before he left."

"Huh. Phil does no good deed without a price."

Dan smiled through gritted teeth, speaking with a voice husky from years of drink and smoke. "Phil's no problem, May. He sticks to my price."

That doesn't sound like Phil. His wallet's tighter than a tick on a dog.

Dan lifted a crowbar off the floor near his foot. "Got some nasty mud on this. Mind if I clean it off in the washup?"

He didn't wait for an answer and swaggered toward the back, ducking his head to get through the doorway and hollering, "Mind what you charge. I know you got a low price for some folks."

She set down his overflowing plate and the bill, charging him the lower price. No sense arguin' with a mean man carrying a crowbar. Still, it irked her. Family rate was for folks outta work or having hard times.

THE BELL ABOVE the diner door jingled as Deputy Sarah stepped in, boots all black and shiny like she'd just got out of the academy. Her pristinely ironed shirt and trooper's campaign hat, set perfectly straight on her head, made her the anomaly in the casual Paris Park sheriff's office. She smiled at May and hooked her hat and coat on the wall. "Mornin', May. What'cha got today?"

"Same's every day, Deputy. Toast, grits and eggs, bacon on the side."

Sarah had once told May privately she didn't mind being called by her first name. May had shaken her head and tsk'd. "These ol' boys don't respect you yet. We help you earn it by using your proper title. One day, you'll see what I mean."

May eyed the police cruiser parked on the left side of the diner, opposite Dan's hauler and out of view from the counter elbow. The sun's gleam off the windshield gave no way to know whether anyone was behind the wheel. Could be that young recruit Tom. Deputy Sarah was his T.O.—training officer. May's late husband Marty had been one in Georgia, his quiet temperament and patience similar to Sarah's.

Sarah sat at the long counter, back to the road, rather than her usual seat at the elbow. If anyone needed to watch the road, it was the deputy. *Something's up.*

May poured Sarah's coffee and looked up in time to see Deputy Tom sprint past the gap between the diner and Dan's truck. He must have gone around the back because he sure hadn't run across the front.

D AN RETURNED FROM the washup, water still dripping off the crowbar. He leaned it against the counter near his left leg. "Morning, Sarah. Working alone today?"

"Not on duty yet."

May set Sarah's plate in front of her and turned back to wipe out the skillet. She preferred cooking on the skillet—one meal at a time. Less stove to clean later. Only when the diner was crowded would she fire up the griddle in the middle. She turned back to the stove and added bacon to the empty skillet, preparing for the next customers.

Sarah poured milk and sugar into her coffee mug—biggest one in the diner—and took a long slug of the result.

May chuckled. "Don't see how you can use that much sugar and not gain weight, Deputy. You're downright a miracle."

"Work it off all day, May. When I'm not working, gotta watch it pretty close."

Dan mopped his plate with his toast and pulled a few bills from his wallet, dropping them on the counter as he picked up the crowbar to leave.

May gulped. Whatever Dan was suspected of, Deputy Tom might need more time. She cleared her throat. "No tip, Dan? I make a good breakfast and serve with a smile."

"Tips are for exceptional service. Want more money? Raise your prices." He stomped out, slamming the door behind him.

Sarah raised her eyebrows at May. "Everything all right?"

"Your deputy. I don't think he got away from Dan's truck in time."

"Nice delay attempt. Thanks."

Sarah's radio crackled and Tom's voice came through. "Whew. Glad the door's got a bell. I hid in the bushes until he pulled away."

"OK. Come on in and tell me what you found."

TOM JOGGED IN and took Dan's vacant seat.

May set a cup of coffee in front of him and said, "Jeet yet?"

Tom leaned into the counter. "No time to eat, May. Got to catch up with Dan's hauler."

May dropped bread in the toaster and cracked two eggs in the skillet, breaking the yolks with a spatula. "You'll take an egg sandwich with you. Dan won't get far with that load. Did you see how low the tires are?"

Tom's confused look when she turned to face him produced a laugh. "My husband was a Georgia state trooper. I know all sorts of tricks and tidbits *and* how to keep quiet."

Sarah nodded. "May's good people, Tom. Good thinking to check out his hauler. Tell us what you saw."

"A boot ... couldn't tell if it was attached. I mean ... to a body. That's as far as I got before I heard the door jingle."

He sipped, then stopped. "Oh, wait. Blood on the edge of the trailer, like maybe Phil was dragged onto the hauler and covered with some rock."

"What's the condition of the side rails. The driver's side looked sturdy, so no reason to flag him down for an unsafe load."

Tom flushed and stammered. "Well ... maybe there's a loose retraining strap on the passenger side?"

May laughed. "You may be green, kid, but you got good instincts. Before you go, Dan washed off his crowbar in the washup. And he said Phil had gone backwoods fishing—alone."

Sarah nodded. "Thanks. Don't run the water back there or use the sink. We'll send someone to check it over."

The deputies' radios crackled. "Sarah, looks like you were right. The hauler's turning east on Old Main. He could dump a body in the woods out past Fish River Lodge. Should we follow?"

Sarah spoke into her mic. "Yes, but not close enough for him to see you. Don't want to spook him and cause an accident. His load's heavy. If it shifts, do a traffic stop. One strap's loose on the passenger side. Deputy Tom and I will be along shortly. Take surveillance photos if he unloads anywhere."

May placed a foil-wrapped sandwich on the counter in front of Tom and waved off his money. "This is on me. You two gave me a nice trip down memory lane with my late husband. Now go get your man."

———— ⬥ ————

A T FOUR O'CLOCK, May turned off the blinking Open sign and locked the diner door. Cleanup was quick. Not too many customers these past few days, not since the police had put out a BOLO on Dan.

She turned out the lights and exited a side door to the stairwell to her upstairs apartment. The plate of leftovers in her hand could sit on the table until she got hungry. It was time for her puzzles. Today would be Sudoku and maybe some crosswords, accompanied by the crackles and commentary of a police scanner. She never let on to anyone that she kept one active up here, a soothing reminder of life with Marty.

It had been a week since Dan had come in and cleaned his crowbar in her washup. Later that day, a deputy had done forensics. Left fingerprint powder and such behind, but May had expected that. Did her spring cleaning in that room the next day.

Deputy Sarah had come for breakfast several times since but said nothing about Dan or Phil. May didn't ask. Diner talk had told her about their fistfight two weeks ago at the pub on the outskirts of town.

The police scanner filled in more. According to the chatter, Dan's story about Phil gone fishing didn't hold water with Deputy Sarah. Her state police training was accorded deference. Maybe the good ol' boys would show her the same respect if her instincts about Dan were right.

Both men were known for arguing and not just with each other. Phil was tight with a dollar and negotiated hard on trade-ins at his dealership. But, Dan? In May's view, he was as worthless as gum on a boot heel.

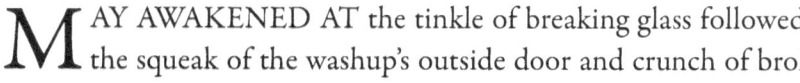

M AY AWAKENED AT the tinkle of breaking glass followed by the squeak of the washup's outside door and crunch of broken glass. She dialed Deputy Sarah. "Ain't nobody gonna rob me and git away without a fight, Deputy. I got a gun and know how to use it."

"Stay put, May. Don't put yourself in danger. I'll be right there, no lights, no sirens, so don't shoot *anyone*."

Hmph! Deputy Sarah lives way on the other side of town.

Moonlight cast ominous shadows across the room as clouds crossed the night sky. May slipped into her slacks and moccasins and threw on a dark Mackinaw shirt. She checked the clip in her Diamondback DB9 pistol, set the safety to off, and crept down the stairs. Halfway down she stopped and peeked out the window. Just leaves and shadows changing with the breeze.

No sounds emerged from the diner, but these walls were thick. She'd only heard the glass break because her bedroom window above the washup was cracked open.

At the bottom, May pressed her ear against the door. Nothing. She pulled out her phone, dialed Deputy Sarah, whispered "Shhh," when Sarah answered, and slid the phone into her shirt pocket.

Crossing herself in silent prayer, she opened the door, keeping her body to one side in the small foyer. Again. Nothing.

She peered around the door frame. Empty stools, barely visible in the gloom of night, lined the counter area. Curt swears and the scuffs of a heavy object being pushed across the floor emitted from the washup.

May crossed to the front door and eased the lock open, then moved to the counter in five strides, her moccasins soundless on the linoleum floor. She stopped for a long breath, then turned at the counter elbow and raised her pistol in the two-handed grip her Marty had taught her. "Stop right there."

Metal clanged against the floor, followed by a shadowy figure.

——— ❧ ———

MAY FLIPPED ON the diner lights, exposing Dan crouched and poised to retrieve his crowbar.

She chuckled. "I can shoot faster than you can pick that up and throw it. And believe me, I got good aim. Taught by one of Georgia's best."

"No need, May." He knelt, hands raised above his shoulders. "I ain't arguin' with no gun."

"Now you're talking sense. Why are you here? Leave something behind, maybe?"

Sweat gleamed off Dan's forehead. The set of his shoulders and look in his eyes said he was calculating how to overtake her.

May shook her head. "They think you killed Phil. Now why would you go and do something stupid like that?"

"It ... it was an accident. We was arguin' and ...." He dropped his head to his chest.

"Keep those arms high, Dan, or I might pull the trigger. It'd be your word against mine. Who do you think they'll believe?"

"Look. May." He glanced around the empty washup, then into her face, his eyes cold and distant. "I got money. Lots. Phil don't need it no more. We could split it. Just don't tell anybody I was here, okay?"

May nodded toward the heavy wood piece he'd pushed out of place and raised her voice. "You dropped it behind the storage bays? Police searched here after you left. Probably found it."

"I'll leave town. Go far away."

"Too late, Dan. I expect them to walk through the front door any moment now."

He grunted. "Expect me to believe that? You ain't smart enough to have an alarm system. I checked when I was back here last week." Hands still raised, he began to stand.

"Don't make me pull the trigger, Dan. I don't want to know what it feels like to kill a man."

"Well, I ain't sticking around to get arrested." As he rose, his hand flashed to his boot.

May pulled the trigger as he threw the knife. Her bullet caught him in the shoulder, and the knife went low.

He lunged and knocked her to the floor, only to be bashed on the side of the head by Deputy Sarah's pistol.

Sarah cuffed Dan and helped May to her feet. "I told you to stay put."

"If I'd a done that, he'd have gotten away, and you'd never catch him for Phil's murder."

Sarah sagged and May grabbed the deputy. "What ...? You're bleeding."

"Dan's knife missed you, but not me." Sarah held onto her left thigh and staggered to a chair at the nearest table.

Deputy Tom and the sheriff rushed into the diner.

"What the blazes?" The sheriff's eyes widened at the sight of Dan moaning on the floor and Sarah bleeding from her wound. "Deputy Sarah. You were supposed to wait for us."

Sarah nodded, her eyes glazing as her head dipped. "I was listening to the conversation. Figured Dan would try to harm May."

May brought a large towel to stem the blood flow from Sarah's wound. She pressed a cold wet cloth on Sarah's head. "I called the ambulance company. On their way." She turned to the sheriff. "Here's my gun. I shot Dan."

TWO WEEKS LATER, Deputy Sarah was at her usual stool in May's diner and had just finished the breakfast special.

May refilled her coffee mug. "When do you go back on duty?"

"Tomorrow."

"Feeling up to it?"

"Sure. I'm ready."

"Good. Make sure you don't skip meals. Body takes a while to heal and needs nourishment."

Sarah nodded and reached for the order slip. May snatched it from the counter.

"Nope. You don't pay nuthin' today. Nasty Dan finally got what was comin' to him. And the sheriff called you Deputy. Today, you get the Family Rate."

Miss Aggie's Pigs

"'MORNIN', MISS AGGIE."

The chorus of baritone and tenor voices greeted her entrance, announced by the tinkling bell above the door. She shut it quickly, leaving the harsh November chill outside, and warmed herself in the fire-lit warmth of the general store.

She nodded to the men gathered around the chess and checker tables, then turned to her business. "Good morning, Fred. I'll have a half dozen pork chops, if you don't mind."

"Are you sure you're dressed warm enough, Miss Aggie? That wind brings a pretty raw chill with it today."

"I'm fine, Fred. I walk briskly, so that keeps me warm."

Fred packaged her pork and added it to the order he'd already prepared for her. "I'll have my boy bring this up to your place after closing today, so you don't have to carry it."

She turned and smiled as young Bill, the county's electrician and deputy, sidled up to her. "Miss Aggie, I worry about you being so alone out there all winter. Do you want me to come by and check the heaters and your furnace? I have some time tomorrow that isn't booked."

"Why thank you, Bill. That would be just fine. I'll have an apple cake and chicken pot pie ready for you to bring home to Georgia. I hear she's not feeling well."

"I don't know how you stay up on everything yet we hardly ever see you in town, Miss Aggie. But you're right. This one's different. Doc says Georgia has to stay in bed until the baby comes."

Well no wonder. If you didn't have her making babies year after year, she might have a chance to recuperate. Give the poor woman a rest! She smiled instead of voicing her thoughts.

Fred came out from the behind the counter with a large mug of hot tea and the two men escorted the wiry woman to a chess table. She sipped as she matched wits with Fred.

"That's mate." When Miss Aggie smiled, her eyes crinkled at the corners and sparkled like a child with a lollipop.

"Another game. I want to redeem myself." Fred bristled at being bested, but always kept trying. "I don't know how you beat me every time."

"Strategy, Fred. You have to think three or more moves ahead to win at this game."

"Yeah, yeah, yeah."

The men hid their smiles at this oft-repeated banter. Miss Aggie was the best chess player in town, probably in the county. Her advanced years had not dulled her wits. Fred's grumbles were offset by his crooked smile, the scar down the side of his face a remnant of Miss Aggie's long-gone husband's short fuse.

"That was a nice ceremony last month, Miss Aggie. Reverend Edgewoods did a nice job, but I was surprised you included Lily Temperance in it. After all, she took Herbert away from you."

"Time heals many wounds, Fred." Miss Aggie did not mind discussing this in front of the others. The whole county knew he'd run off with Lily, the town's former postmistress.

"Herbert never was much of a husband, God rest his soul. Come to think of it, he wasn't much of a man, either. He was a cheat and a fool. I'll never forgive him for what he did to the people in this town. Running off was the best thing he could have ever done."

The men nodded their agreement, with a few low-voiced remarks. Miss Aggie sipped the last of her tea. "Well, I have more errands. I better be off."

She left amid the good-byes and Tom promising to send his son over to chop more wood in preparation for winter.

———— ⁓ ————

FROM THE GENERAL store, Miss Aggie stopped at Reverend Edgewoods' home next to the church. "Good morning, Ruth. Is your husband in?"

"Oh, Miss Aggie. How good to see you. Yes, he's just finished writing Sunday's sermon. Why don't you come in and have some tea."

"Oh, thank you, but no tea. If I have any more I swear I'll float away. I had quite a large cup at Fred's. I just want to make a donation to the church." Miss Aggie followed Ruth into the pastor's office off their entryway and waited for Ruth to fetch him.

"Miss Aggie. How good to see you."

My goodness. Do these people have nothing better to say than, "How good to see you." Ever since the ceremony. This town lacks imagination. Or they're all being so polite because they think I'm some sort of saint who'll crack under the pressure of her man being officially declared dead.

"Reverend, here's a check for the church. I know I've already paid you for the ceremony, but this is extra. It's my way of thanking you, and the town, for treating me so well despite Herbert."

The Reverend's eyes widened when he looked at the check. "Miss Aggie, it's too much. I can't take money that you might need. It wouldn't be right."

"No. No. It is right. Herbert was a vile man who caused a lot of harm. If his insurance money can do some good, then I'm trusting you to know how to use it."

She pushed the check back into his hands, stood, and left.

———— ⁓ ————

HER FINAL STOP was the beauty parlor for a cut and blow dry, a rare treat she permitted herself today. She exchanged recipes with Edith and Millie and caught up on the town gossip she'd missed since the ladies bridge club met at her home two weeks earlier.

Edith, in the chair next to her, was a real estate broker and always tried to get Miss Aggie to consider moving into town. Everyone in the parlor listened to the conversation, as Miss Aggie didn't visit often.

"I can't imagine staying in that isolated house Herbert moved you into. We worry about you, Miss Aggie. That road is impassible in the winter and almost too rutted to drive on in the spring."

"It's my home, Edith, and I'm comfortable there."

"Don't you worry about being stuck there all winter, cut off from everything? Isn't it lonely?"

"Isolated isn't the end of things, Edith. I have my preserves, the cow and chickens for milk and eggs, a huge freezer of meats, and a root cellar full of vegetables from my garden. As for lonely, I have my books ... hundreds of them. They keep me great company."

Barbara Jean stopped in the middle of drying Miss Aggie's hair. "Tell me, Miss Aggie, why did you ever keep those pigs Herbert bought? I thought you hated them. Aren't they awful ... so dirty and smelly?"

"Well, Barbara Jean, they're hogs now. That's what they're called when they mature. As for dirty, that's just mud. They roll in it to cool off because they don't sweat. The mud protects them from bug bites, too. They're actually quite clean animals and don't roll in their own 'you know what.'

"Truth is, I've grown to like having them around. They eat just about anything, and half the town helps feed them with their food garbage. Pretty soon I'll send them off to the butcher's knife. There'll be fresh bacon and pork to go around the whole town from those two. Then I'll start over with the babies they've given me."

I T WAS LATE afternoon by the time Miss Aggie arrived home. She stoked the fireplace and went out to feed the animals, stopping last at the hog pen.

"Well, Mr. Herbert and Ms. Lily, it's almost time to say goodbye forever. There's no one looking for your namesakes and only I know what I've named you two. I was waiting for the insurance check—wanted to be sure no one would ever come looking for my long-lost husband and his mistress. And why should they? There's no trace. After all, hogs will eat just about anything."

After the Rush Fades

"DID YOU SEE THIS?" Peg's red curls bobbed as she slid the company newsletter across the table. Sally shuddered when she saw the headline and photo. She pushed it back to Peg.

"No way." Sally's furtive whisper was hoarse as she balled her hand into a fist. "That woman is morally and ethically bankrupt!"

"Go on. Read the whole article." Peg pushed the newsletter back to Sally, who read while Peg talked. "I don't know exactly why you despise your manager. But I wanted to see your reaction to this."

Sally's face reddened as she read.

> Mrs. Helene Powers will be awarded the Triskelion Award at the company annual meeting in two weeks. The company's prestigious award is given annually to the employee who represents the highest standards in three areas: business ethics, integrity, and responsible management.

She stopped reading and grabbed Peg's arm. "C'mon, we can't talk about this here, and now I can't eat."

They left the newsletter on the table. Sally called Bruce to join them at a nearby deli. The lunch crowd now gone, Sally could speak freely to her two friends. She had difficulty keeping her anger in check as she revealed what upset her about Mrs. Powers being selected for the award.

Bruce set his glass down, his eyes widening. "YOU started the investigation on Briggs Holding, Inc.? I did the final report but knew someone else did a lot on it before Mrs. Powers gave it to me."

"No. It wasn't me. Well, yes, I started it, although Mrs. Powers doesn't know that. It was Doug, your predecessor, who did the bulk of the work. I only helped. I'm sure she gave you a cleansed version of his research."

Confused, Peg looked at the two others. "You mean this is all about the Briggs report? There was an internal investigation ..."

Sally pushed her drink aside. "Okay, details coming ... but you can't repeat this to anyone, or I'll be joining Doug in the unemployment line. Peg, remember how Doug's job went vacant for something like four months? Then, all of a sudden there was budget money to replace him with Bruce? Sorry, Bruce, you may not have known about that. I like you. I really do. But Doug was a good worker and my friend.

"Anyway, that whole budget thing really bothered me. I knew it wasn't true. I felt responsible 'cause ... well, I should have been the one to bring the problem to Mrs. Powers in the first place." She sipped her cola.

Peg slipped her a napkin to clear her misting eyes. "Sally, don't think for a minute that you're responsible for Doug. *Fish Face* did it. For whatever reason, good or bad, it was her, not you."

She turned to Bruce. "Bruce, *Fish Face* is what my department calls Mrs. Powers. Sally's group doesn't dare 'cause they're afraid they'll slip one day and call her that to her face."

Sally smiled at her friend's loyalty and dabbed her eyes before putting her thick glasses back on. "I'll start at the beginning. I discovered what I thought were accounting discrepancies. I wasn't sure, though, so I went to Doug. He's loads more talented in financial stuff than me and checked them out. I said he could bring it to Mrs. Powers' when he was done." She looked down at her hands. "I took the easy way out 'cause the less I have to deal with her the better. She's a *kill the messenger* kind of boss."

"Yeah, I've been seeing that lately." Bruce pulled out a pen and began doodling while Sally continued.

"Anyway, she told Doug to write up a report. Then he was laid off a few months later. That budget excuse didn't seem right to me ... and I kinda felt guilty. I thought maybe he was laid off because of what his research revealed."

Peg glanced at her watch and gasped. "Oh gosh, I have to get back. Can we finish this later? I want to hear *more*."

———— ⁕ ————

THEY MET AFTER work over chips and beer at Sally's apartment. Peg perched on the edge of the couch while Bruce sat in an easy chair, doodling again. Sally started with details neither of her friends knew—things the official Briggs Holding Report didn't include.

Peg interrupted. "Wait a minute, *Fish Face* was in cahoots with Briggs? Did Doug know that when he showed her the accounting discrepancies?"

"No one knew. Doug dug deeper, and updated me a few times, after giving Powers his initial findings. We both thought some of the approved projects didn't seem solvent and wouldn't produce income even long term. We didn't know, then, that she was in cahoots with Briggs."

She paused to pop some chips in her mouth, followed by beer, then continued. "Doug must have said something that made her realize he was still digging, and she created an excuse to let him go. After he was laid off, I started digging—*on the q.t.* I didn't want to suffer Doug's fate. I found emails, kickback schemes, all sorts of stuff that pointed to *Fish Face* working with Briggs."

Bruce raised his finger to halt Sally's recital. "Wait a minute. Emails? Kickbacks? There's nothing about that in my report."

Sally flashed a quick smile and leaned forward, lowering her voice even though they were in her apartment. Bruce and Peg leaned in as well, their heads almost touching over the coffee table as Sally spoke.

"That's because you didn't have everything. A friend at my last job taught me a few hacking tricks. I got into her system and found emails between her and Briggs. They both knew the projects weren't solvent."

Sally let them digest her words while she munched chips, then said. "Here's the real deal. Briggs is paying her kickbacks for inside information so his bids will win. Years from now, when the insolvent projects don't produce profits, she'll blame someone else."

Bruce said, "How come those emails didn't show up during the investigation after my report?"

"She must have erased them to make it look like Briggs was working without her help. Thank goodness I had copied them while snooping. But I haven't known what to do with them since."

She leaned back in her chair and sighed. "I've spent months trying to figure out a way to secretly tell the company without risking my own job. It's been eating me up. I have to stop her from getting that award."

Bruce looked almost as angry as Sally had when she first read the article. He stopped doodling. "It's not right, her getting the company award for integrity when she's cheating her way to it. She's risked all our jobs ... the whole company."

He tossed the pen and pad on the coffee table. His doodle image was a fish, with Mrs. Powers' face; he'd added horns rising from the hairline and a wolfish grin across the face. "Now I'll never get that big bonus for my work on the report."

Sally and Peg exchanged glances. Peg broke the uncomfortable silence. "Bruce, my department prepared the graphics and final formatting of not just the report but her memo to the president. You'll never get that bonus because your name isn't anywhere on the documents, just hers. It's probably why she's getting the award."

Bruce's husky voice trembled, and he focused on the coffee table. "Ha! I asked her about my bonus, and she said it was delayed. Then she had an excuse about how it has to go through channels. Last week, she said she's not happy with my work. I saw that kind of runaround at my old job ... was stupid to think it wouldn't happen here. I've put my resume back out there, ya know?"

He straightened in the chair, eyes shining with moisture. "She's been stringing me along for months! But now, to find out that she's behind the very scheme that *her report* revealed to corporate. She shouldn't get that award. Sally, what can we do?"

———— ❦ ————

TWO DAYS LATER, Peg and Bruce parked in the alley behind the strip mall on Fourth Street and knocked on the back door of Unit #3.

"I feel so silly, sneaking around like this," Peg whispered.

Sally opened the door and motioned them inside. "Come in, quick. Did anybody see you leave work together?" She ushered them into a workroom in the back of a shop.

Bruce answered. "We were careful ... very careful. No one saw us." He put his laptop bag on the counter and sat on a work stool while Peg sat on another. Bruce stared at the open racks filled with computers and related equipment, most in various stages of disassembly. "Wow, what is this place?"

Another knock at the back door made them both jump. When Sally calmly walked over to it, Peg brushed the curls off her face and sat back down, smoothing her skirt. "I guess this clandestine stuff is making me a little nervous."

Sally opened the door and admitted Doug. His shorts and T-shirt were a stark contrast to the others' work attire. Sally shut the door after a glance outside. Doug placed two steaming pizza boxes on the workbench and grinned back at Peg's stunned smile. "Hi. Long time no see."

Sally introduced Doug to Bruce and then answered Bruce's earlier question. "This is my friend's computer shop. He's letting us use the back room for our project. I asked Doug to join us because he's suffered the most from *Fish Face*."

She sat on a stool and nabbed a slice of pizza. "I have a plan. We've agreed we should do something to prevent her from getting that award. BUT ... we shouldn't." She waited for them to calm down. "Stopping her isn't enough. It won't expose her ... what she's done ... to everyone in the company. Before I say more, we all have to swear that everything we see, do, and hear from this point forward is secret. Tell no one ... even if you're caught."

Hours later, fueled by self-righteous indignation and anger, they had fine-tuned Sally's plan like a video game. *Fish Face* had earned a new name; the four mutineers were ready to push *Captain Bligh* onto a lifeboat while they sailed away to victory.

———— ❦ ————

THEY WORKED AT the shop many evenings over the next two weeks. The award ceremony followed the same formula every year—a flashy intro with upbeat music, images only while the honoree is introduced, approaches the podium, and speaks, then back to music and corporate images for the ending. Using the previous year's video as a guide, they created alternate files to insert into this year's video.

Knowing they'd have only minutes to get the desired effect, Sally and Bruce selected the most damning emails. Peg created blown up overlays of critical statements from them. Doug read these onto the audio track, his voice altered for protection.

The mutineers' video would run off their laptops. Sally's shop-owner friend wrote a program to keep the laptops in perfect synchronization. If one failed or had to be closed, the others would continue playing the same media file. He hacked into and created a hidden connection in the closed-circuit loop that ran the company's media booth, then taught Doug what to do when the event began.

At work, Peg monitored the network drive daily, jumping at the slightest sound or approaching footsteps. Sally tried to keep her friend calm and made sure they ate together every day. Two days before the event, the compiled and approved video was placed in the folder she monitored. She copied the video and the raw files used to create it onto a flash drive.

That evening and the next, the four mutineers played and replayed the video on a large monitor in the shop. Peg updated the fonts, colors, and background of the files she had created with those used on the approved video. Everyone gave advice and corrections to make the final product perfect. Sally inserted Peg's files into place, and they recompiled the video with their version. By ten p.m. on the night before the event, they agreed the video was ready.

They high-fived before leaving the shop. Finally, they'd see justice done.

THURSDAY—THE ANNUAL company meeting. Early that morning, Peg replaced the original video with the mutineers' sabotaged copy, its file creation date altered to match the original. At 9:30 a.m., employees filed into the multi-purpose cafeteria and auditorium. Chatter filled the air—about work, kids and pets, clients, and more. The serving area had been transformed with staging, chairs for executives, and a podium. Behind that, an enormous screen had been lowered from the ceiling. Auditorium seating replaced the lunch table layout.

The room's high-tech wizardry was managed from a control booth in the media room near the entrance. Video cameras mounted from the ceiling captured and streamed the annual event to satellite locations and important customers. The entire event would be uploaded to the company website afterward.

Sally sat behind a pillar on the empty running track high above the auditorium, ready to slip away if anyone approached. Peg and Bruce were similarly hidden—Peg in the deserted kitchen, Bruce in the maintenance storeroom near the control booth. They opened their laptops and initiated the synchronization program. From his van in the parking lot, Doug monitored the video feed through the closed-circuit loop on his laptop.

Minutes before the event began, the technician left the control booth for a final check of the stage microphone. Sally sent Doug the preplanned text message. Filtered through layers of fake IP addresses and other hacking methods to escape detection, Doug took control of the booth and disabled the technician's board. He redirected the automation program to run the laptops' video.

Now the mutineers merely had to watch—the video, for security, for anything that would signal they might get caught. Their hope was that the video would be over before anyone could track down the problem. If someone did get close to a mutineer, the others could remain in place, letting the video continue while the first scurried away. If no one was caught, it would appear as if the control booth had been running the network version.

When company president Phil Beckman took the stage, Doug set the video in motion. Music and images settled the crowd. Music faded out and Beckman welcomed his employees to what he assured them was a stellar event and the beginning of another strong year for the company. His address said nothing of the quiet layoffs that had occurred with greater frequency over the past seven months, nor the clients who shifted allegiance to competitors. It was all roses and champagne, according to his speech.

He introduced Mrs. Powers and noted her achievements. "Her meteoric rise through the ranks, moving our company forward, keeping us strong in a time of fiscal uncertainty elsewhere, are unprecedented in our company history."

He spoke of her prowess as a manager and how she'd saved the company millions by discovering several risky business deals the company was then able to avoid, proving her *a shaker and a mover*. Sally groaned. She texted to her co-conspirators, "Ack, this makes me want to throw up."

Mrs. Powers' approach to the podium was accompanied by images demonstrating her successes, including the cover of the Briggs Holding report. She wore her red power suit and high heels rather than the usual loose dress and sling-back shoes. Bright lipstick flattered her face, softening the harsh lines her staff knew so well. Beckman pinned a white rose to her lapel and handed her the coveted trophy while the crowd clapped.

"Good afternoon. I am just thrilled to be here with you today. I hope you share my joy at such an event—" The microphone stopped working. She stalled for a moment, then tried to resume. She tapped the microphone, smiled to the audience, and turned to Beckman, who rejoined her to help.

Next, emails between her and Briggs displayed while the audio track read the overlays. She turned to the screen as more damning phrases were displayed and read. Her face turned ghostly. Her smile drooped into a frown. She swayed in her high heels, clutching the podium for support. Beckman held her up and looked at the screen, alarm on his face, then hurried her off the stage. The executive vice president, usually a minor player in these events, screamed at the technician to turn everything off. Nothing the technician tried on his disabled board worked.

The vice president shouted for managers to clear the room, but the most damning emails, overlays, and audio had done their damage. The audience shifted from stunned silence into a quiet roar of chatter. It seemed to delight a number of employees who, once they were away from the watchful eyes of their managers, laughed and joked as they returned to their workstations. Peg, Sally, and Bruce closed their laptops and joined the dispersing crowd of colleagues, as if they'd been with them the entire time.

T HE FOUR MET at a remote bistro after work. Elation flowed, but they kept their voices low.

"That was genius," said Bruce. "Did you see the look on her face when she heard the audio? I'd love to be a fly on Beckman's wall right now. She's got a lot of explaining to do."

Doug nodded. "It was perfect—precisely planned and executed. Thank you, Sally, for that vindication."

Sally kept looking around as they talked until Peg poked her and said, "Hey, stop that. Keep it cool, ya know, like you kept telling me at work."

Sally nodded but continued glancing around throughout the evening. She went home, exhausted but unable to sleep. She sat in a chair by the window overlooking the swimming pool of her apartment complex. The moon's reflection on the water reminded her of that day in the shop when they had talked giddily about pushing Captain Bligh—Mrs. Powers—into a lifeboat by exposing her crimes to the entire company.

It seemed longer than two weeks since this began. What had felt like a video game that first day had become very real. *I wonder how the real mutineers, who set Captain Bligh on the high seas in only a lifeboat, felt as they sailed away?*

Waves of guilt swept her elation aside, engulfing her in reflection. Her stomach churned while her intestines began to burn. Like a tide changing direction, she was flooded with contradictory emotions. She placed her glass on the coffee table and covered her face with her hands, moaning quietly in the night.

What madness had infiltrated her soul that she could judge someone morally and ethically bankrupt, then publicly humiliate that person? Were her hands so clean that she could be judge, jury, and executioner? Had she just become as ethically bankrupt as Mrs. Powers?

She slept not at all that night and little for the next week. Something tore at her, ebbing and flowing in the darkness of her soul.

———— ⁊◌⁊ ————

PEG AND BRUCE didn't understand when she met with them days later to discuss her remorse. They urged her to apply for one of the positions that would surely be available in the upward shuffle as the company moved someone into the now-disgraced and fired Mrs.

Powers' position. That would make her feel better, they said. They'd accomplished their mission. You deserve to move up, they said. You've been overlooked too many times—by Mrs. Powers herself. Sally wouldn't budge.

Her shining triumph over evil had tipped her into the abyss of soul searching, only to find she was flawed and undeserving of praise. She'd done a terrible wrong that could never be forgiven. She would never tell anyone, she promised, wouldn't get them into the trouble that would cause. Heartsick, she needed to start over.

A week later, she typed "personal" in the box asking Reason for Leaving, packed her belongings in a small box, and walked out the company door.

Mutineer no more.

A Grave Development

"GRACIE, I'M HOME." George placed his briefcase on a chair and his keys and driving glasses on the kitchen table.

"In here, dear. Bring me that crepe paper on the counter, would you?"

George stopped short when he saw Grace on a ladder in front of the living room window. "Honey, your arm. You know the doctor said to take it easy."

"Oh, pooh. That old fart. He'd have me in bed doing nothing all day. My arm has healed fine. See?" She raised her arm, then continued to drape crepe paper below the top edge of the window. "And the rest of me recovered even more quickly."

"Well ... all right. But you don't want to overdo it."

She looked down at him and burst into light laughter. "Worry wart. If it's fine for me to clean and cook, a little ladder isn't going to break me."

He handed her the crepe paper and stepped back. "Nice effect. But why are you decorating inside?"

"George Arthur Fulton, please don't tell me you've forgotten we're hosting the Halloween block party this year. After all your begging and pleading to get me to agree last year." She shook her finger, but he knew from her smile that she was teasing.

"I lost track of how late in the month it is. Boy, I must be more wound up about work than I thought. Want a drink?" He poured one for himself and looked up from the wet bar when she didn't answer.

She was staring at him. "George, is everything all right at work? You said last night that it was. But now you don't sound so sure." She stepped down from the ladder and took his drink. He poured himself another and they settled in easy chairs.

"Honey, everything is fine, or, at least it will be."

"What do you mean it will be? Either it is or it isn't, isn't it?"

"Not exactly. Peter, the new manager, has been riding me pretty hard. I was afraid he was going to fire me. I think I'm in the clear, though. He left for Chicago this afternoon. Everything should be fine when he gets back." He rubbed his forehead and gulped his drink, letting the liquor burn its way to his stomach.

"Are you sure? I know it's been rough, what with Frank gone and their bringing in Peter from Chicago to take his place. But honey, if you lose this job, I can find one. I miss working. Wish I'd never let them talk me into retiring." She set her drink on the coffee table and shifted in her chair to face George.

"There's been a development, Grace ... about Frank. The police are questioning everyone. They even brought in a forensic accountant. It seems a lot of money went missing when Frank disappeared."

George refilled his drink and paced the living room. "I'm the best salesman on the team but my commissions kept dropping. Remember I told you about Frank taking one of my good accounts and turning it into a house account, so I no longer get commissions on it? What I didn't tell is that he's done it a dozen times over the years."

"No. And I thought he was such a nice man."

"At first it was only one or two. Then, he got greedy. Every time I'd get one going strong and it looked like we could put money aside to take a trip—Boom! He'd convert it ... so he said. What he really did was make it one of *his* accounts."

"That's dreadful. How did you find out?"

"After Frank had that renovation done on his house last year and bought a new boat this spring, I figured out his password and got into his accounts. He was careful, always waited a few months, then transferred the *house account*," George made air quotes with his fingers, "to himself."

"Oh, you poor dear. No wonder you've been so distracted. Here I thought Frank was so thoughtful, sending me flowers after my stroke. He even visited me in the hospital once. You never really know people, do you?"

"No, I guess not. He was stealing my money *and* telling me to work harder. Well, I was—to improve *his* lifestyle."

"I wish you'd told me this sooner. I could have cut expenses on our end."

"Oh, no. We're all right. It's just that we've never moved ahead, never been able to buy a boat or redo the house. Heck, with what he's made off me, we could've bought a bigger house and still put money aside for trips." He moved back to the bar to prepare another drink.

"George, do you really want a third one? I know you're upset, but we have so much to do ...."

"You're right. I'm on autopilot." He bent down and kissed her cheek. "I'll change my clothes and get the grill ready. Steak tonight?"

"Chops. All defrosted and salad's ready, too. We can eat on the deck if you'd like."

"Yes, that would be nice."

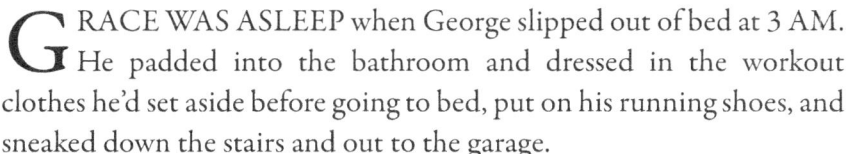

GRACE WAS ASLEEP when George slipped out of bed at 3 AM. He padded into the bathroom and dressed in the workout clothes he'd set aside before going to bed, put on his running shoes, and sneaked down the stairs and out to the garage.

Good thing I oiled this door last week. He slipped inside and grabbed the flashlight by the door. The shovel was on the other side, hung neatly beside the rake and other tools. The spare tarp was folded on a shelf beneath the pegboard that held hand tools. Grabbing the shovel and tarp, George moved around to the back of the house where he'd already loosened a large patch of soil and began digging.

"George, is that you?" Grace's hushed whisper made George drop the shovel. He spun around, finally seeing Grace's head poking out from their second-floor bedroom window.

Grace stuck her head out further. "It *is* you. Honey, what are you doing?"

"Shush, you'll wake the neighbors. I'll be up in a minute."

George returned his tools to the garage and joined Grace, who'd come down to the kitchen. "What were you doing out there at 3 AM?"

"I couldn't sleep. Thought I'd get a head start on planting hidden items for the block party. The theme is still pirate's booty, isn't it?"

"Yes, dear. But we don't have to bury things in the middle of the night. I've told a few of the neighbors we're digging up the yard to plant new trees and bushes. Rachel is sending over her two teens on Thursday to dig holes around the yard except where you prepared last week for the new brick fireplace. By Friday everything will be ready."

George grunted in acknowledgment. His stomach, however, did a quick rollover as they returned to bed, and he lay awake the rest of the night.

THE MORNING PAPER splashed Frank's photo across page one. The top-of-the-fold article and photo sensationalized the story. Grace slid the paper to her husband. "George, this article says Frank embezzled a lot of money. Was that from your accounts?"

"Oh no, stealing our accounts would give him commissions. He must have stolen company funds, too. I guess someone leaked the auditor's report, 'cause we weren't told about this." George gulped the last of his coffee and picked up the paper.

He skimmed the article and whistled. "Wow, over a million bucks. Guess they'll look real hard for him now."

"It says he bought a plane ticket to Europe, with final destination Kazakhstan."

"Huh. Good luck getting him back. No extradition with the US. I guess Peter won't have any trouble believing me now." George's stomach relaxed for the first time in weeks. *Only one more thing to take care of.*

That night, Grace woke each time George tried to sneak out of bed. "George, settle down. I'll never get any sleep with you tossing and turning."

------- ⟨≈⟩ -------

WEDNESDAY AFTER DINNER, George crushed a sleeping pill and slipped it into Grace's cocktail. She declined. "I think the nightcap's making me a light sleeper. I'm going to bed without one tonight.

He silently cursed but smiled and sent her off to bed. "I'll sleep on the couch, Gracie. Maybe I'm what's keeping you up."

She returned minutes later with pillows, a sheet, and blanket. "You're so thoughtful, dear. It's what I love about you." She kissed him goodnight and went to bed.

George repeated his trip to the garage for his tools and sneaked into the yard. Again digging in the patch he'd loosened a week earlier, he struck the hard plastic of a tarp and carefully dug around the outline. He pulled the wrapped form onto the spare tarp, dragged the heavy load into the garage, and hid it beneath the tool shelves. *Whew, that's done. I can rebury it after the party.*

G EORGE TOOK FRIDAY afternoon off to help Grace with last-minute preparations. They buried the last of the party treasures in the yard, pleased with how much work the twins had done the day before. They planted clues in the house and yard and set up signs that could help or confuse the treasure seekers. Their last preparation was to hide items inside the house for party goers who didn't want to dig for their treasure.

That evening, food and drinks flowed as neighbors brought various dishes and more drinks. At midnight, Grace distributed the clues to each couple or single and told them to, "Go find the pirate's booty."

George had borrowed enough shovels so everyone who wanted to dig outside could play along. He stayed in the kitchen talking to friends while Grace went outside to observe the treasure hunt.

George nearly spit out his drink when, minutes later, he heard someone shout, "Hey, everyone, look. I think I found Blackbeard's body! Somebody help me pull this thing out."

He raced outside in time to see Grace looming over an unburied tarp.

She said, "Congratulations. Yes, that's supposed to be Blackbeard. You get the grand prize tonight."

Several people rushed over and began pulling the tarp from the hole, while others cleared away dirt. George was too late to stop them and nearly fainted when the tarp unfolded and revealed the face of his former boss.

Grace turned to George as he grabbed her arm and swayed. "George, are you all right. You don't look well."

T HE POLICE RELEASED the party goers to their homes. Two officers remained outside with George and two others were questioning Grace in the living room.

"Honestly, I didn't know what was in the tarp. The twins found it in the garage. I let them in on the party secret and had them bury it. Thought I'd surprise George, too."

"And you're sure no one else has been in your yard lately ... even late at night?"

"Oh, no. George is the only one who's been out there late—. Oh, my. That means ...."

"Yes, Mrs. Fulton, we believe your husband murdered his boss and fixed the books to make it look like he had embezzled corporate accounts. We planted that story in the paper to give us time to prove it."

Grace looked at the officer. "You never really know people, do you?"

A FTER THE POLICE arrested George, Grace checked her jewelry box where she'd hidden the key to a locker at an out-of-town gym. A week ago, she'd registered under a false name and paid cash for a one-month trial. The workout clothes she'd bought at a consignment shop weren't the locker's only occupant. There was also a large gym bag holding more than a million dollars cash she'd found when she first discovered the tarp in the garage. George would have a hard time describing how the money had disappeared from the tarp that still held Frank's body.

She lay down to sleep. Dear, sweet George. I found your ticket to South America so easily. And all that effort digging the fireplace pit to bury Frank's body? I didn't make it easy for you to unbury it before the party, did I? You never really know people ... do you?

Danger on the Black Double Diamond

ELBOW ON THE TABLE, chin resting on her palm, Beth indulged in her daily coffee shop ritual: watch, listen, speculate. Except today, she was in the dining room of a crowded New Hampshire resort two thousand miles from her Arizona home. The line to get in snaked out of view—skiers eager to fuel up before tackling the fresh powder that had swept through overnight.

Staff hustled to bus and replenish the tables, creating a cacophony of clattering dishes and voices, yet no one rushed Beth in her booth at the far end. She shielded her eyes against a burst of sunlight, enhanced by the picture window on her right, and reviewed the trail map as she ate. Green circles, easiest; blue squares, intermediate; black diamond, difficult; double black diamond, experts only. *Should I try blue today?*

A couple in line held hands and flirted. *New hookup, just getting intimate with each other?* That fortyish woman rubbing her bare ring finger. She stopped when a younger man joined her. *Cheating on hubby? There goes his arm around her back.* The woman shifted, leaned away. *Recently divorced and uncomfortable with dating?*

What would Beth suggest if any of them wrote to her "Ask Annie" advice column?

The line moved forward, revealing a woman alone, no smile, not looking around. Recent breakup, like me? Oh, why did Bruce have to pop up in my head? I'm only twenty-five and can do better. I can hear him now, "Beth, honey. Mind your own business. You know what happens when your imagination runs loose." Hmph. Who does he think he is? There was just that one time. So what if it involved the police and turned out to be nothing?

MAKEUP CRINKLED IN the hostess' smiling face as she approached Beth's section. Fifty-ish? Wrong shade of red hair dye for her skin tone and age. Trying to be twenty again?

The hostess dropped menus at the booth ahead of Beth's and stepped aside for a couple to seat themselves. The woman slid in, leaving Beth with a view of thick black curls escaping from the bottom of a brilliant red ski hat with a white pompom. The man sat facing Beth.

Hmm ... she's maybe late thirties, from the little I saw. Sixty-ish for him. They don't come off as romantic, and he's dressed for corporate, not skiing. Lawyer and client?

A fierce gust startled Beth as it whipped last night's powder against the window and across the deserted deck that edged over the side of the mountain. *Maybe that'll die down this afternoon. I'll read by the fire this morning.*

A twenty-something waitress took the couple's order, then refilled Beth's coffee. "Hitting the slopes before the storm sets in?"

"Storm?"

"Nor'easter."

"But it's gorgeous out there." Beth pointed to the puffy clouds skimming across the blue sky, as if chasing warmer weather. Another gust swirled snow across the deck. "Well, if you don't mind the wind."

"On its way. Could be a bad one. Mount Washington is already socked in." The waitress pointed southeast.

Beth craned her neck in the same direction, but the mountain in question was under heavy clouds. "Is that bad?"

"Not from New England, huh? Heavy wet snow, pushed by strong winds. Just when you think the storm's over, it cycles back and hits you again." She smiled and dashed off toward the kitchen with her order pad and empty coffee pot.

Red Hat's low, throaty voice caught Beth's ear. "You can't talk me out of it, Fred. I've thought about it for months."

The man shook his head. "Why mess with a good thing? She's your golden goose."

"I'm tired of her. I'm finishing her off this weekend."

A chill ran down Beth's spine. She leaned forward, pretending to pick something out of her omelet, to look at Red Hat's face but curls obscured her features.

He lowered his voice. "So what'll it be? Gun's too loud. Knife's messy. Maybe poison like Concord?"

Beth's drumming heartbeat drowned portions of the woman's response.

"... like an accident ... knock her off a ski lift." The woman paused. "Nah, someone might see."

"Push her off the trail into a ravine?"

"That works. In fact, I know the perfect spot."

He frowned, shaking his head. "I hope you know what you're doing."

She nodded. "I guess you'll head back to Manchester now that this is settled."

When the couple left, Beth dug bills from her wallet, left them on the table, and dashed off to catch up. *Perhaps I can get a glimpse of her face.*

There. Exiting through the front door. Beth ran outside and into organized chaos. People with luggage. Loaded ski racks. Snowmobiles skimming across the road. No Red Hat. Well, plenty of red hats, but none with that white pompom.

Beth's shoulders sagged, and she shivered in the brisk air. *Did I really hear that? What would Bruce say? No, forget him. I'm here alone, someone's planning a murder, and I need to figure out who so I can warn them.*

— ∽◦∽ —

BETH FIDGETED IN the plush chair by the fireplace and set the romance novel down for the fourth time. *How could she find Red Hat in a sea of skiers and prevent a murder?* Without the hat ... well, she'd recognize that husky, long-time smoker's voice if she heard it again.

At eleven o'clock, she ate an early lunch, bundled herself against the cold, and rented skis for the afternoon. With each run, she skied a different trail, then watched others swoosh into the bowl-shaped basin and lumber back to the lift. No Red Hat.

By late afternoon, Beth had skied all the blue trails. Her knees and thighs ached from making tighter turns than she needed on the green trails. Snow from several tumbles had worked its way under her coat. *How does one remain upright on two sticks that don't always go in the same direction?*

Visibility decreased as ominous clouds dropped fat, wet snowflakes. At the basin, she shivered while wolfing an energy bar. *I should go inside where it's warm and rethink this. Wait! There's Red Hat.*

Beth shuffled into the snakelike lift line and hopped on the chair when her turn came. Focused on Red Hat three chairs ahead, she ignored the man text messaging next to her and leaned sideways to see ahead. They were almost at the top before he put the phone in his pocket and said, "You seem anxious. First time on a lift?"

"I'm fine ... just looking for someone. Thanks for asking."

She scurried off the lift and followed Red Hat, who sped out of sight. The steep trail was too narrow for Beth's lazy zigzag pattern. Heart racing, she made several clumsy turns before swooshing over a low embankment bordering a thicket of shrubs and trees.

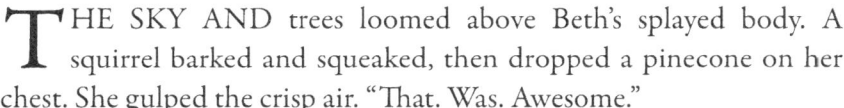

T HE SKY AND trees loomed above Beth's splayed body. A squirrel barked and squeaked, then dropped a pinecone on her chest. She gulped the crisp air. "That. Was. Awesome."

One leg was wedged into a small bush, its ski dangling from the security strap around her ankle. Her other leg was buried in snow. She couldn't tell if there was a ski attached or not. Testing her muscles, she sighed with relief. "I guess nothing's broken."

With each attempt to get up, she sank deeper, an upturned turtle on a cold sea of snow. "For cryin' out loud, I'm stuck."

A male voice startled her. "Hello there. Are you hurt?"

Rescued. "I ... uh, no. Just stuck." She leaned her head backwards into the snow. A blurry upside-down figure was making its way toward her. *No, silly, you're upside down.*

"Hold on. It'll take a minute to get to you." The stranger from the ski chair trudged into focus. "Hello again. You're lucky these bushes broke your fall."

He moved around to face her and had her lift and bend each arm and leg. "Nothing seems broken, although you've lost one ski. How do you feel?"

"Kinda dumb. I took the wrong trail."

"Ya think?" They laughed together. "Can you stand if I pull you away from the bush?"

"Let's try."

He moved behind her, gripped under her armpits, and pulled her upright. "You okay now?"

"Uh-huh."

He removed his goggles and hat. Curly brown hair and green eyes. Tanned or natural dark skin? Who cares? He's gorgeous and I'm just plain clumsy. She swayed slightly.

"Whoa, there." He held onto her arm while she steadied herself. "Sure you're okay?"

Beth's heart hammered a staccato beat in her ears and her legs wobbled. "A little shaky."

"Adrenaline. You'll be fine in a few minutes. I'm Roger."

"Beth." Her face flushed. "This trail is a bit steep for me. I lost control." *What must he think of me?*

"I'll find your other ski and we'll go down together ... slowly."

He returned minutes later with her other ski, and they lumbered out of the thicket to the trail. He stood after reattaching her skis. "Do everything I tell you, okay?"

She nodded. The air was eerily quiet except for his occasional instructions and a few "good job" comments. Thick snowfall obliterated any tracks ahead, and Beth's legs were lead by the time they reached the base. Roger waited while she turned in her rental skis.

She began to thank him again when he asked, "How about a drink? We can get to know each other better."

"Sh ...sure." Oh boy, my face is probably beet red.

B ETH SNAGGED TWO leather wing chairs by the fireplace. Roger brought two beers and a bowl of pretzels from the bar. "Okay. Now that we're comfy, tell me what you were doing on the double black diamond trail. You obviously aren't a novice, but don't belong on the expert ones."

"I'm embarrassed to admit I was in a hurry and didn't check the markers."

"Let's hope you don't make that mistake again."

They toasted to that and chatted. He grew up near the mountain, worked the ski patrol for many seasons, and skied all over the world. This mountain, he said, was a home away from home. She told him about her advice column and coming here after a breakup, omitting details. It was time to forget the fights with Bruce, her high school sweetheart who was dropped from the football team and then scraped by with the minimum credits to graduate. Their on-and-off relationship since then was punctuated by his berating her advice column while he couldn't hold a part-time job collecting scrap. *Covering his insecurity? Why did I stay with him so long? My insecurity?*

"... so I wondered if—"

Beth shook her head. "Sorry. My mind wandered. Could you repeat that?"

Roger smiled. "I talk too much. You must be tired."

"Oh, no. It isn't you. Sometimes my mind grabs a stray thought and takes me with it. I apologize."

"No need. Do you have dinner plans? The pub food is excellent."

"Sounds nice. I'd like to stay put for a while."

"They'll come over to take our orders soon. By the way, why were you in such a hurry to get down the mountain that you didn't look at the trail marker?"

The dreaded question. But Roger feels ... safe. She leaned forward and lowered her voice. "I was following someone who's planning a murder." *There. She'd said it. Bruce would be laughing at her.*

Roger furrowed his brows and matched her whisper. "A murder? Are you sure?"

She bobbed her head. "Uh-huh. At breakfast I overheard a woman telling her friend. I tried to follow, see where she was going, but lost her in the crowd out front."

"That is scary. But ... how do I say this? Are you really sure? I mean, most people don't discuss murder plans in a crowded dining room."

"Go ahead. Laugh. That's what my ex would do." She wiggled farther back in the chair and swallowed more beer.

"I'm not your ex. I believe you think you heard that, or you wouldn't have tried to follow her. It was a dangerous thing to do."

"I know that now. But I had to try."

He cocked his head and raised an eyebrow.

Beth let out the breath she'd been holding. He hadn't laughed her off, and his warm, brown eyes invited trust. "A close friend ... in high school ... there were four of us who did everything together ..." She took another pull of beer. "She was pregnant ... told me she wanted to kill herself. I didn't believe she was serious."

Roger leaned forward and wiped the tear that trickled from the corner of her eye. "I'm sorry."

"It's haunted me ever since."

"Because you did nothing?"

Beth shook her head. "Worse. I did nothing and *lied* ... told the police and her parents I had no idea why she did it. But I knew ... and should have done something. Ever since, I haven't been able to stand by and do nothing. Life is too precious."

"You could tell the authorities what you overheard."

Beth blushed. "Well, once or twice since then I misread a situation and ...."

Roger settled farther into his chair and nodded, remaining silent.

It's as if he understands, so unlike ...

"Tell me the whole conversation you overheard."

A T HER DOOR after dinner, Beth heard the low, husky voice from this morning. She hurried down the corridor, but doors banged shut before she turned the corner. *Missed her again. Well, she's on my floor. That's a step forward.*

In her room, she sat at the tiny desk and grabbed the notepad by the phone, then paused. *Am I chasing ghosts? No. Roger agreed it sounded as if the woman was planning a murder and that it wasn't her first. Make a list of what I remember, like a sleuth. Can I remember more than the hat? Let's see ...* she scrunched her eyes and visualized Red Hat on the lift. Long white skis with multi-color diagonal stripes across the front tips and crosshatched across the back. Red pants that matched her hat. *What color was her jacket? Why didn't I get a better look at her face?*

She examined her paltry list. *I'll try again in the morning.*

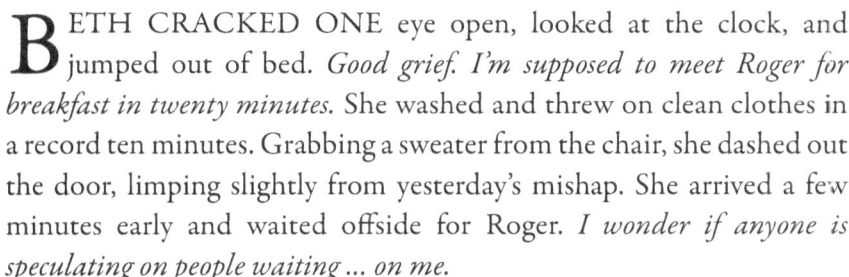

BETH CRACKED ONE eye open, looked at the clock, and jumped out of bed. *Good grief. I'm supposed to meet Roger for breakfast in twenty minutes.* She washed and threw on clean clothes in a record ten minutes. Grabbing a sweater from the chair, she dashed out the door, limping slightly from yesterday's mishap. She arrived a few minutes early and waited offside for Roger. *I wonder if anyone is speculating on people waiting ... on me.*

A steady snow fell against and piled onto the outer window ledges on the far side of the long dining room. It was pretty as long as you were inside and warm. Roger arrived and the hostess led them to the booth Beth had occupied the day before. She rushed into a seat, her back to the dining room.

Roger cocked an eyebrow.

She looked around to make sure they were alone. "Okay, before you ask. I grabbed this side of the booth because Red Hat sat right behind this seat yesterday. If the hostess tends to seat people at the same tables, we might get lucky."

"You've given this some thought."

She blushed. "Look. Last night I wrote down what she was wearing on the lift." She searched in her pocket. "Damn. My key and the list are in my other sweater. Now I can't get back in my room."

"The front desk will give you another key."

"Oh, that's another thing. I heard her last night. She's on my floor." She crinkled her lips. "Not sure which room yet."

"Describe the woman to the desk clerk and ask what room she's in." He glanced at his menu, then set it on the table. "Look, Beth. You want to do the right thing. But are you putting yourself in danger?"

"How can I do nothing? I'm the only one who heard her. Well, except for her friend, and he's gone."

RED HAT HADN'T shown up in the dining room, and Roger left for the slopes. "I promised to help my patrol buddies make sure everyone's off the mountain by late morning. That's when the worst of the storm should hit. If she's getting in last-minute runs, I'll follow. Meet in the lounge at one?"

Beth nodded. *At least he takes this seriously.* She remained inside and searched the main floor—lobby, lounge, and gift shop next to the dining room. Red Hat wasn't anywhere. The desk clerk recognized Beth and gave her another room key but would not disclose information about other guests. She nodded when he said she'd want her privacy respected the same way.

Returning to her room, she propped the door open to hear anyone in the corridor. Walking back and forth to the elevator did nothing to ease her anxiety. *This is getting me nowhere.*

She grabbed a book and her list and returned to the same fireside chair in the lounge she'd sat in yesterday. Several times she got up and walked through the almost deserted lodge, then returned to her spot by the fire. Was everyone out on the slopes?

Soon, the fire that had seemed so inviting was too warm. She moved to a sofa farther away. The TV over the bar was set to a news channel that updated weather alerts every ten minutes. *Sheesh, they make it sound like the end of the world. Meanwhile, something bad is going to happen right here.*

Stragglers drifted in, their chatter an insect-like background to the commentary running through her head. I can't wait for Roger. I'll check the other buildings, see if she's in the ski shop or spa. I have to find her, talk to her, see if what I heard was real.

——— ∽ ———

B ETH FELT SILLY putting on extra layers but heeded the words of the weather forecasters. An icy blast knocked her sideways when she opened the main door to the lodge. She staggered, bent her head forward, and struggled into the wind, taking a circuitous path to avoid a large snowdrift. In the shop, someone asked the clerk about the forecast. Beth listened for the low, throaty voice. No luck.

Outside again, the storm blew Beth toward the lodge, then battered her in another direction. Large drifts blocked her access to the guide ropes between buildings. *Should I go back? No. Gotta see this through. I won't have another life on my conscience.*

The wind screamed in her ears and snow obscured her vision. Staggering to remain upright and gulping for air, she reached the spa. The door wouldn't budge. Then someone pushed against the door from the inside. Beth grabbed the handle again and pulled, her head low against the wind. The door burst open, depositing two women bundled for the weather, their hoods pulled tight against the wind.

One said, "We're the last. And the power keeps flickering. You might get trapped in there."

Beth thanked her and began the return trip with them. The wind pushed her forward, and she almost fell. The second woman grabbed and held onto her arm. Another gust made them all stagger and the second woman said, "We're like drunken sailors returning from shore leave."

Beth gasped. *Red Hat.*

Red Hat peered at Beth's face. "Easy there. Are you all right?"

"Fine. Yes. Just startled." *Startled to be caught in a blizzard with a murderer helping me. What was I thinking?*

The two women positioned themselves on either side and locked arms with Beth. Together, they fought their way through the storm. With a burst of energy, the three plowed through a drift Beth never could have managed alone and reached the entrance. They staggered into the lobby and dropped onto a wooden bench positioned over grates that captured shedding snow. They shook off their hats as the clerk came over and asked, "Are you ladies all right? Did you see anyone else out there?"

"Yes, we're fine, now that we're inside." Red Hat said. "We were the last to leave the spa. We checked. And made it here in one piece, literally. If we hadn't hooked arms, one of us might not have made it." She laughed.

Ironic. She seems so normal, yet she's planning to murder someone.

RED HAT—MAGGIE—and Patrice introduced themselves and invited Beth to join them for lunch. She explained she was meeting Roger at one o'clock.

Patrice said, "That's perfect. I'm gonna change and take a nap, but first I'll make reservations for one-thirty. Okay?"

Beth agreed. *How can I sit through lunch and pretend I don't know Maggie is a murderer? Should I just come out and tell her what I know? Ask her? What if it's Patrice she's going to kill? Oh, I wish Roger were here now.*

She returned to her room and propped the door ajar while removing her boots and outer layers. Maggie's voice boomed from the adjoining corridor. "Look. I told you last week, I'm done with you."

Beth jammed into her moccasins, sneaked down the hall, and peeked around the corner. Maggie's back was to Beth. A woman about Beth's age faced them both—Beth pulled back when she saw a red ski hat with white pompom in the woman's hand. *Which one did I see on the lift?*

Their venom-laced stage whispers carried around the corner to Beth. The younger woman's husky voice was tight. "I made you what you are today. You won't get away with dumping me."

"Do what you want. But you're history."

"Oh, believe me, we're done, just not how you think. This isn't over."

Beth heard one door slam, then another. *What was that about?* She walked back to her room, closed the door, and lay down to think. She drifted off to a disturbing dream with a car rushing down the mountain slope while she tried to ski away from it. More tired than when she'd fallen asleep, she took the bath she'd skipped that morning, dried her hair, and met Roger on time.

"Storm's fierce. We had to help a few people off the mountain. No Red Hat though. Why the glum face?"

"She was here the whole time. Her name's Maggie, I think. Or maybe it was the other woman. Oh, I don't know. I'm all mixed up now."

"Maggie? Other woman? What happened while I was gone?"

"I know. It's so confusing. Anyway ..." Beth recounted her morning adventure, the lunch invitation, and the overheard conversation in the corridor.

Roger smiled. "Maybe you'll learn more over lunch, clear up the confusion."

L UNCH BEGAN WITH cocktails that calmed Beth's frayed nerves. Roger introduced himself, Beth and Patrice said what they did for work, and Maggie said, "I write murder mysteries."

Roger raised an eyebrow at Beth and asked Maggie, "What are you working on now?"

"Oh, I'm starting a new series and need to end the other one. My long-time heroine will become the victim."

Beth nearly choked on her drink. "How?"

Maggie said, "I don't like to talk about a work in progress. Roger, what do you do?"

Roger talked about his ski patrol days. Beth ate and nodded several times but didn't hold on to any of the conversation. *I did it again. I got involved in something that turned out to be nothing. At least I didn't call the police on her, but I might have if the lines weren't downed by the storm.*

Their main course had just arrived when two men in ski boots clomped in and approached Roger. They spoke in low tones and showed him a cell phone. He handed the phone to Beth. "Isn't this the person you described to me? The one on the lift yesterday?"

White skis with multi-color diagonals and crosshatches and a red hat like she'd seen on Maggie and the woman in the corridor. The only difference was the ski pole sticking out of the woman's chest as she lay in the snow.

Patrice took the phone and put her hand over her mouth. "Norma!"

"You know her?" asked one patroller.

"Yes. We're in the same smokers-cessation program. Terrible addiction. We get together, then go our separate ways. But if anyone feels the need, there's someone they can call. Several of us came up this weekend. I bought us all these red hats. We were going to have a party tonight." She dabbed the tears moistening her eyes.

Maggie took the phone with a shaking hand. "How did this happen?"

"Not sure. Found her off the double black diamond trail, partially buried in snow. We wouldn't have spotted her except for the red hat. Poor woman. We're trying to find out who saw her last."

Beth's mind replayed the scene from the corridor. The angry woman who'd accosted Maggie had snow clinging to her hat as if she'd just come in. She was the right size to have been the person Beth had overheard at breakfast and seen on the lift. "If she's the woman I overheard in the restaurant—"

Maggie interrupted. "Do you know something about this?"

"Yesterday at breakfast, a woman in a red ski hat with a white pompom spoke about killing someone by pushing them off a ravine here this weekend."

"That was me. I was talking to my agent about my book—how I'd kill my heroine."

The second patroller interrupted. "We found this woman near a ravine. Are you saying you didn't do it?"

"No. I was in the spa with Patrice. She," Maggie pointed at Beth. "found us there around ten-thirty. I didn't ski today."

Beth asked, "Maggie, who was the woman in the corridor with you after we got back from the spa? The one with the same outfit as ..." she pointed at the phone on the table.

"Norma's daughter Cherise, my assistant ... former assistant. She proofed my manuscripts, suggested edits, that sort of thing. But she was unreliable and seemed ... unstable. She began demanding co-authorship and royalties. I fired her last week."

"What was the argument about?"

"The same thing every day for the past week—demanding her job back. I'd said even Norma agreed with my decision. Yesterday afternoon when she saw me, she claimed to have come up with some convoluted demise for my character—" Maggie gasped and put her hand over her mouth.

When she spoke again, her voice trembled. "I told her *how* I would do it. In the corridor this morning, she seemed ... I don't know ... frantic? Cherise has a nasty temper, but ... murder ... her own mother?"

The lead patroller took back the phone. "We'd like to speak with her. Until the roads re-open, ski patrol and resort security are the closest thing to any kind of authority. We need to find out what happened."

PATRICE AND MAGGIE canceled the evening party and left for their respective rooms. Roger went with the ski patrol group to check equipment and prepare for re-opening the lifts, while the two who had interrupted lunch searched for Cherise. The raging storm kept everyone else except staff indoors for the rest of the day.

Beth had a glass of wine and read by the fire in the lounge, restarting at the same page after each time she set the book down. Another glass of wine and two hours later, she startled when the book slid from her lap and thudded against her foot. She had no desire for company or the background chatter of others in the lounge and returned to her room and ordered room service.

She slept poorly that night, waking every few hours to mixed memories of her high school friend's and Norma's deaths. Rising early, she dressed and paced in her room until it was almost time to meet Roger for breakfast.

On her way to the dining room, Beth stepped outside to see how much snow had been dumped overnight. She wrapped her arms in a self-hug, her sweater little help against the bitter cold, as she spoke with a staff member taking a smoke break.

"With every lull in the storm," he said, "we clear the walkways between buildings. Forget about the parking lots. Every road in or out is blocked. Drifts, downed trees and power lines—it's a mess out there."

She nodded, teeth chattering. "I'm impressed the resort has power and food."

"Have our own generators. And with the forecast's prediction, we stocked up for a multi-day lockdown. Nor'easters cycle back and regurgitate. Good for the resort, though. Lots of fresh snow. But the spa's temporarily closed ... uses too much power."

Relieved that the man seemed to feel this storm was all very normal, Beth went inside and found Roger waiting for her at the dining room entry. "Sorry I'm late. Stepped outside for some air."

"In that?" He pointed to her sweater. "Brave. It's well below freezing. But it brought nice color to your cheeks."

The hostess led the blushing Beth and chuckling Roger inside. She stopped in the almost-deserted dining room and asked. "Same booth?"

"Sure. Why not," Beth answered.

Beth slid into her original seat that faced the large room and asked Roger, "You don't mind, do you? Occupational habit, observing people."

"Not at all." He studied the menu. "What kinds of questions do you get for your advice column? What are your favorites to answer?"

"Are you trying to distract me from yesterday?"

He set the menu down. "I'm interested ... in you ... what you do. But, yes, maybe also a distraction."

"Thanks. That's nice." She bridged her hands and set her chin on them, elbows on the table. "The feeling's mutual."

ROGER FINISHED EATING and left to help the ski patrol check and mark the trails before the lifts would open to the public. He'd work with them all day to supplement their small crew, as one patroller was with the security guard searching the resort for Cherise.

Beth lingered over her coffee, scribbling notes on the back of the list she still carried in her sweater pocket. Maggie's room and cell number, given to Beth during yesterday's lunch, were at the top of page. Maggie had said to call if she saw or remembered anything about Cherise. *Why would Cherise murder her own mother? Did she mistake Norma for Maggie?*

Service was slower than usual, the waitstaff's drawn faces showing the strain of working extra shifts because their replacements couldn't get there. Diners frowned and shook their heads. *Probably just been told the lifts won't be open for a few more hours.*

One couple argued with a waiter over their check, and the manager intervened to soothe frayed tempers. Only the hostess seemed unaffected, her smile ever present and her pace brisk. *She's probably more used to this than the younger staff. Could provide an interesting article for a slow column day.*

More diners straggled in, and Beth returned to her room, dressed for the cold, and headed outdoors. First stop, the ski shop. Not that Cherise would be there, but Beth had to do *something*.

Then she tried the gift shop. It was much larger than the shop inside the resort, and Beth was distracted by the many New England tchotchkes, graphic T-shirts, and other paraphernalia designed to entice random purchases. She shook her head and refocused. *Find Cherise.* She gave no thought to what she'd do if or when she found her.

Outside the gift shop, Beth hesitated and shielded her eyes from the sun's glare bouncing off the snow-covered scene around her. She pushed on, pausing near the cement benches facing outward from a circlet of baby Scotch pines. On her first day at the resort, she'd sat there to take in the hustle and bustle of arrivals and departures. Today, there was no hustle and bustle, and the trees were a ghost family huddled under the snow.

The spa was next. Worth checking, even though she'd been told it was closed. *It would be the perfect place for Cherise to hide.*

The padlock on the front door nearly deterred her. The storm had blown hard in one direction, leaving a large gap in the snow on the other side of the building. A set of bootprints disappeared around the back. *Security might not have checked there.*

Beth pursed her lips, then followed the tracks that led to several crates stacked against the back wall beneath a not-quite-closed window.

Emergency lighting revealed little inside the dark room as Beth pushed the window up and climbed through the narrow opening. Feet dangling, she risked the short drop to the floor. "Oof."

Her landing and voice echoed. Otherwise, there was stark silence. She rose from the floor and turned on her phone's flashlight. Tiptoeing across the room, Beth noted the racks of spa towels and supplies. There was nothing to stand on to exit through the window, and the front door was padlocked from the outside.

If Cherise had come in through the window, couldn't she have used a lobby chair to climb back out? If she was still in the spa, where would she be? A trickle of sweat ran down Beth's back. She unzipped her coat and stuffed her gloves and hat into its deep pockets.

Apprehension became her companion as she opened the door. She winced when it creaked. A flood of thoughts hammered her—two repeating as she crept down the hallway towards the sounds of sniffling and babbling. *What will I do if she's here. If she murdered her mother, she'd have no qualms about killing me ... would she?*

B ETH FOUND CHERISE huddled in a corner of the sauna, feet curled under her on the floor, rocking, crying, and talking to herself. Beth used her phone to record the woman's condition.

Cherise looked up, and her eyes widened. "Who ... who're you?'

Her slurred words and the discarded whiskey bottle on the floor added to Beth's suspicions about why Cherise hadn't left the spa. Beth moved closer and asked, "How long have you been here?"

"Huh?" Cherise's eyes narrowed and she leaned forward. "You!" Her head lolled then snapped up. "Saw you ... the corridor ... spying on me ..." She blinked rapidly and swayed.

"Did you follow Norma down the trail? Did you two have a fight?" Beth turned on her phone's recording app.

Cherise blurted what Beth suspected. "It was supposed to be Maggie. She always skied the toughest trail." Her head lolled again. "Not my mother. Oh, what have I done?"

She fell into a sideways swaying rhythm, jabbered incoherently, then would raise her head and reveal portions of the argument with her mother on the edge of the ravine.

Beth teared at the anguish in Cherise's voice.

"I begged mother to get my job with Maggie back. She refused, said I need counseling. We fought."

More sobs and tears. "I-I grabbed her. We struggled ... and ... in my rage, I didn't see mother. I saw Maggie ... and stabbed her with her own ski pole."

Cherise collapsed into herself, sobbing, then blacked out. Her pulse was thready, and Beth feared she might be slipping into alcohol poisoning, something she'd learned about when answering a question for her column. She removed the empty bottle and used a chair to wedge the spa door shut behind her. The security door she exited through triggered an alarm, and the security guard and ski patroller met her halfway back to the resort.

THAT EVENING, THE smoker's cessation group, with Beth and Roger as Maggie's guests, gathered in a corner of the lounge. People recounted stories of Norma's wit and her funny strategies for quitting smoking.

Partway through the memories and toasts, Maggie raised a glass to Beth and said, "You've got spunk, kid, I'll give you that. I'd wondered why you were headed for the spa in that storm. You didn't save Norma, but you tried to prevent a murder. And then you found Cherise ...."

The group raised their glasses and toasted Beth. A chill ran down her spine. *One person kills herself. Another kills her mother. Life can be fragile.*

Roger took Beth's cool hand in his warm grasp. "Cherise's confession should put her in prison for a long time. It took guts to do what you did. Scared but determined, you pushed fear aside to help a perfect stranger."

Beth sighed and closed her eyes. *Roger feels right. Even if I never see him again after this weekend, I am whole. No more put-downs—from myself or anyone else. And I'll never again be afraid to seek or speak the truth.*

Cheating Death

"GEEZ, KID. WHAT'D YOU have to go and shoot him for?" Willie pushed Bobby away from the clerk's body and out the door of the convenience store.

"'Cause he was gonna shoot me! He pointed that rifle right at me." Bobby's voice shook as much as his hands.

Willie took Bobby's gun and stuffed it in his jacket pocket, almost crushing the map he'd just stolen. The other pocket held a pint of whiskey and three packs of cigarettes, none of which he'd paid for. He looked around the empty parking lot and surrounding street. "Waving that gun around, you'll have every cop in town on us in minutes. I already got all the cops in Ohio chasing me. Find us a car. We gotta get outta this state fast."

Minutes later, Willie jimmied open the door of a '94 Honda Accord parked outside an auto body shop. He leaned over, unlocked the other door, and hot-wired the engine before Bobby was in the car.

For a big man with a hefty beer belly, Willie moved faster than the younger, skinny, tow-headed Bobby. Heading northwest on Route 27, Willie lit two cigarettes and handed one to Bobby to help calm his nerves. Bobby coughed on the first few puffs but kept smoking.

Willie drove just under the speed limit, stopped at all the stop signs, and slowed down as he passed groups of older youth in gaudy Halloween costumes, capes and sheets fluttering in the late-evening breeze ... anything to avoid looking like he was in a hurry to get away. The teens must be returning from the youth center party he'd seen advertised in the convenience store. *Typical small-town event. Keep the kids out of mischief so they won't grow up to be criminals like me.*

Both stiffened when two police cruisers screamed past, headed toward the store they'd just robbed—and Bobby had shot the clerk. Sweat and tears trickled down Bobby's face.

Why'd I ever hook up with this baby-faced piece of trouble? Willie hoped his nephew's stupidity hadn't hammered the final nail in his coffin. He flicked his cigarette out the window and turned to Bobby, his voice weighted with years of smoke and whiskey. "What you gonna do now? Piss your pants? It's over. You did it. Learn to live with it."

"That's easy for you to say, Uncle Willie. You been in trouble all your life. Me, I never done nuthin' like this. Never. It's like Momma always said. 'Uncle Willie is trouble. Stay away from Uncle Willie.'"

Willie kept his eyes on the road and ignored the growing whine in Bobby's voice as he talked through his tears. "Why'd you give me a loaded gun? You said it wasn't loaded ... it was just to scare people. Well, here's a news flash. It scared someone. ME. Now I've killed somebody and I'M GONNA DIE." He broke down in sobs.

Willie said nothing to console him, just kept driving. Tree-lined streets with homes and businesses became large stretches of farmland. Highway 27 offered few turnoffs and little traffic this late in the evening. Willie stepped on the gas, eager to get away from Ohio and all the trouble he'd been in there throughout his life.

Start over, that's what I need to do. Get outta this state. By now, cops'll be hitting the highway. He turned left onto an isolated westbound street. Crossing the north/south railroad tracks, he figured he was close to the Indiana border.

Bobby stopped crying long enough to ask, "Where are we, anyway? I never been this far away from home. Where we going?"

"Goin' nowhere and everywhere, kid. I'm wanted in Ohio, so we'll cross the line up ahead into Indiana. But shooting that clerk this close to the border? Well, you made it a little bit tougher for me to get away from my past. So we'll—Damn! We're almost out of gas. Kid you have brought me nuthin' but trouble since I picked you up at your Momma's funeral last week. I don't know why I bothered."

He steered the car deep into a cornfield before it stopped on its own. "This'll hide it a while. Stuff that loot in the backpack and strap it on. We walk from here."

Cornfields on both sides offered a place to hide if anyone came down the road, which ran straight as far as they could see. They followed it, eventually turning south with the road. A few hundred yards farther, another road intersected. Willie looked around. Southeast led to a nearby farm. Northwest, farther away but in the direction he wanted, were the silos of another farm.

Willie didn't care about Bobby's sore feet and headed northwest. There wasn't enough moonlight to read the map, and the stiff breeze would blow out matches. They could hide in a barn and rest while he checked how close they were to the border.

He cautioned Bobby, "Sound travels far when there's nothing to block it. And see that small house ahead on the right? It's close to the road. We don't want anyone hearing us. Stay on the paved surface and keep quiet."

The two advanced in silence to the farm ahead on the left, but no barns were visible from the road. They took shelter between several metal silos and the large electrical unit that seemed to manage them. It was enough cover for Willie to light a match and check his map.

"The border's close, Bobby—walkable. But it's all farmland. The closest town is some place called College Corner, a bit north. From there, we can hit the county road. It goes straight west and meets the north/south highway near Liberty, Indiana. The farther away we can get from the border, the better."

Bobby nodded, his mouth stuffed with food, swallowed and said, "I'm sorry I caused so much trouble ... shooting that man. I was scared, Uncle Willie."

"Yeah, kid. I know. First time's the worst. Gotta shake it off, though. Let's rest. Then maybe I can find a car that'll get us there quicker."

WILLIE WOKE, THE half-empty whiskey bottle in his hand and Bobby dozing nearby. *Strange, I don't remember drinking. I always remember drinking. And I don't drink in the middle of a getaway.* He shook off the prickly feeling along his neck and stretched to warm himself, then scouted around the farm, using the silos for cover.

Set back from the road, the large farmhouse was dark, and several vehicles were parked alongside. Parting clouds revealed a building on his left. He headed for it.

A voice *in* his head stopped him mid-step. His ears heard nothing but crickets and bullfrogs.

"Willie ... Willie Collins. I've come for you."

"Who ...? What ...?" Willie completed his step and turned his head in every direction. Flattening his back against a silo, hand on the gun he'd taken from Bobby, he inched around the silo, expecting to find a farmer with a shotgun. *But this farmer knew my name. How ...?*

"Willie. Turn around."

Willie whirled to face a cloaked figure, its face unseeable except for grinning teeth. Taller than Willie. Taller than anyone he'd ever seen. The figure shook its fist.

Willie shivered as nausea washed over him. Teeth chattering, he summoned his courage and asked. "Who ... who are you? What do you want?"

"Why, Willie, I want you." The figure smiled, showing yet more teeth, and raised one arm. It's bony, clawed hand reached for Willie.

He stepped back and fell on his behind, stomach jiggling upon impact, eyes glued on the apparition, which chuckled at his misstep. "I've been looking for you. You're on my list. Taking that man's life moved you up ... to tonight."

"Wait! I didn't ... I didn't kill him. Bobby did. My nephew Bobby. He shot the man."

The apparition chuckled again. "Do tell. You gave him the gun, told him it wasn't loaded. You are responsible for the clerk's murder. And here you are, selling out your sister's son, the boy you swore you would protect if anything ever happened to her. You are quite a man, Willie. You'll do just fine in my entourage."

The apparition reached out again. Willie pressed himself back into the dirt, unable to let out the scream that sought release. As suddenly as it appeared, the apparition vanished.

Bobby ran to Willie, who lay shaking and swearing. Bobby helped him stand and they returned to their temporary shelter.

"What happened, Uncle Willie? You were talking real loud. You could'a got us caught."

"You ... you didn't see it? You didn't see that *Thing*?"

"What thing? You were talking to the air. Your shouting woke me up, and I went to find you. What happened?"

"Never mind. We gotta get out of here. This place is ... well, never mind. I ... I gotta change. Give me a minute."

Willie walked away with the backpack and changed his pants and undershorts, swearing the whole time. "Bloody hell, blaming me for Bobby's stupid mistake." He swapped out the items in his discarded pants, looking at the time on his burner phone. *Twelve-ten. Twelve-ten AM. It's morning. That* Thing *said "tonight," but it isn't tonight any longer. It's a new day. I just* cheated death.

When he returned, Bobby asked why he seemed so cheerful. Willie smiled as he answered, "It's just my lucky day, dear nephew ... new lease on life, that sort of thing. Let's clean up and not leave any clues that we were here."

He picked the lock of the storage building he'd seen earlier, took two full gas cans, and put them in the back of a truck—one with no alarm—parked beside the house. Breaking the collar lock and setting the truck in neutral, he and Bobby pushed it to the road. Willie hot-wired it and set off for the Indiana border. "Man, this is too easy. Like my new lease on life has turned my luck."

He searched the radio for a suitable station while driving fast over the country road. "What'sa matter kid? You keep lookin' at me funny-like."

"I never seen you like this, Uncle Willie. Well, ain't seen much of you the past ten years. But all week you've been this grumbly kind of person and now ... you're ... happy? I don't get it."

"I was in the joint most of that time. It gets to ya. Not much to be happy about when you're in the joint or on the run. Since I been out, well, I'm on the run again, ya know?"

Bobby still stared at him. "Yeah, but somethin' happened tonight. Somethin' you're not telling me. You were talking to yourself back there. And you looked *real scared.*"

"Me? Scared? Yeah, maybe. At first. But then ... then I looked at the time, boy, the time. Everyone's got a date with Death. You never know when it's comin' but it is. But what happens when Death comes and the time slips by? What if your day is today and Death is late? Can you cheat Death? Do you die or do you live? I just found out the answer, Bobby. And the answer—What the—"

Willie swerved to avoid hitting the apparition in front of the truck. It swerved with him, and he drove off the road into a tree, narrowly missing the sign that signaled their passage into Indiana.

The apparition chuckled. "No one cheats Death, Willie. You and Bobby were on my list for Halloween Day. When you crossed the border, you crossed time zones. Twelve-thirty AM in Ohio is eleven-thirty PM in Indiana ... and still Halloween Day. Welcome to my entourage."

April Fools

I KNOCKED A BUILDUP of February slush off my boots at the Campus Security entrance and scanned the conference room through the window partition. For the first time since I'd started the job in mid-January, the entire Rucker College security team was on time. The college bell tower struck noon as I entered and distributed the schedule for March into April 1999.

Officer Anthony stood and jabbed his finger on the schedule. "None of us can be off on April Fools' Eve, Chief. It's the busiest night of the year."

I motioned for him to sit.

"Yeah," said another, "and the next morning, we're stretched thin with the aftermath, especially moving cars in the parking lots."

"Moving cars?" My voice squeaked.

"If there's two empty spots between cars, the students wedge a small one sideways between them. We have to track down one or more the other car's owners."

My meeting wasn't going well this morning. "I see. And we can't stop this from happening because ...?"

Anthony stood again. "We can't be everywhere at once, Chief. Dispatch gets calls all night about attempted purse snatchings and simple break-ins. Nothing of value gets taken, but we gotta check. We're at one end of campus, pranks at the other. No matter where we go, they're somewhere else." He sat, mustached face twisted into a scowl, and fiddled with his pen.

Why he worked at a college campus when he didn't seem to like students ... they must delight in tormenting him each April first.

I grabbed a marker from the white board. "What do we know about who's behind these?"

Beth, our receptionist, dispatcher, and all around *go to* person said, "We can't prove who the ringleaders are because they wear Halloween costumes and masks and scatter before we catch up."

"But you do know?"

"Yes, and this year will be the worst." answered a woman's voice from the rear. I shifted right to see better. Perkins. Tiny, smart, and seemed to get along with everyone. Potential for leadership.

I waited, one wrist extended, palm up.

Perkins' face reddened. "Oh, sorry. Blue Moon. Full moon's bad enough, but a Blue Moon on April Fool's eve ... all bets are off. Each group will try to outdo the other."

Beth said, "Frank Flutes is the muscle on heavy stuff like the cars."

I wrote on the board: Frank Flutes—cars.

Soon, my white board held almost a dozen names and a long list of pranks, with four ringleaders: Flutes—cars. Nickie Bottoms—dorm carnage. Peter Quince—staff offices. Tom Snout—the capstone prank.

No one had real evidence, just fleeting glimpses of students scattering from the scene of their latest "crime." My squad would be exhausted by the time the rest of campus staff arrived for work on April Fools' Day.

M Y TEAM EXPLAINED that Snout's capstone prank was carried out with the skill of a military unit. Two years ago, in the quadrangle formed by the administration building, the library, and two classroom buildings, the costumed students had re-assembled a dorm room, right down to the still-asleep student in the bed. Last year, they'd relocated the statue of founder Robin Goodfellow to the middle of a cornfield. It had taken a crane to restore it to the quad later that week. The administration still didn't know how the students had moved it and couldn't anticipate what Snout would dream up this year.

Anthony stood again. "We should hire extra security to beef up our staff that night. We need a strong counter-offensive."

He couldn't see the eye rolls from several officers behind him, two of whom had warned me he'd bragged at the staff Christmas party he'd get the vacant chief's job.

I nodded, "We can talk later," and motioned him to sit. Turning back to the board, I hid my relief that others also found him annoying.

Anthony scowled whenever someone sounded as if they admired the students' ingenuity. I could appreciate the tricks, having lived on a college campus myself roughly twenty years earlier. But my days of keggers and cramming all night for the next day's lit exam had since been supplanted by police work and off-duty efforts to prevent juvenile incarceration. I needed to curb this tradition without resorting to extremes.

We scheduled a special shift beginning at 10:00 p.m. on March thirty-first. The most fleet-of-foot staff would patrol the campus. I held two officers in reserve to report for the 7:00 a.m. shift, while everyone else would be in the office that night to respond to calls. "I live close enough to walk here through the south campus and get an idea of what's going. I'll call in anything I see."

"They listen in on our channel," Officer Anthony said.

I didn't want a lecture on our communication system. "We'll figure something else out for that night. For now, it's business as usual."

THE NEXT DAY, Beth and officers Anthony and Perkins joined me to discuss April Fool's Eve preparations and what they knew about the ringleaders.

Perkins cleared her throat. "I figure Peter Quince has a set of master keys 'cause his group gets past all the locked doors. Most secretaries know now to open their desk drawers carefully because some will have been turned upside down with a piece of cardboard holding everything in place until you pull the drawer out."

Beth added, "Nickie Bottoms is popular with everyone. She gets almost straight A's and tutors students in math and science. Her innocent, *what me?* face belies the prankster within."

I hadn't played games in years, but a game this was—our best guesses about what students would do against their guile and cunning. Short of hiring extra guards or expensive or militant ideas put forward by Anthony, we planned out everything we could think of to avoid major pranks and finally catch them in the act.

I said, "You'd think in a small Midwestern town like this someone would see them pulling the outdoor pranks. Could the locals be in on it?"

"Maybe," said Beth. "There isn't a lot of *town and gown* friction here. Students tend to keep their mischief on campus and our presence brings money into the community."

Anthony offered to bring in a few 'Nam veteran buddies to "keep things under control."

"That might cause a backlash against us. I'll talk with the town police chief and see what he thinks about the pranks. We don't want any trouble between the college and town." If only I felt as confident. As a newcomer, I wanted to tread lightly and permit the town's chief to offer help that night.

Two days later, the town police chief's comments and bemused face said he thought it was all pretty funny, as long as it stayed on campus and not in town. I left his office and, in case anyone local was helping the students, drove two towns away where I bought a set of eight walkie-talkie units.

The next day I set them to a low-use channel and distributed them to the teams of two that would be patrolling that night. We tested them from different locations and discovered I could reach the campus from home. I kept one and gave the mate to Beth.

Ready.

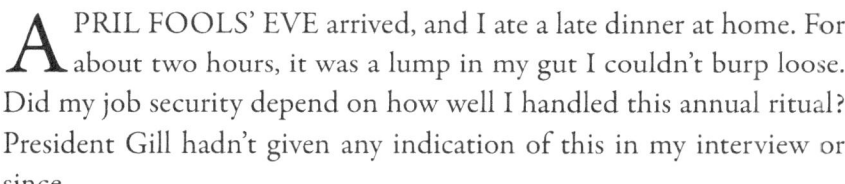

APRIL FOOLS' EVE arrived, and I ate a late dinner at home. For about two hours, it was a lump in my gut I couldn't burp loose. Did my job security depend on how well I handled this annual ritual? President Gill hadn't given any indication of this in my interview or since.

My first meeting with him had been my final job interview in his office. The opulent, carved oak desk, cabinets, and wall-to-wall bookshelves held books, a plaque, and several awards. The office was Monet to the Picasso of my former city police station. The tiny amount of plain wall spaces held several posters. He'd indicated a leather chair by the coffee table as he sat in another. The chair swallowed my small frame into the bowels of a strange new world. *Run*, squeaked a voice in my head.

A poster near the window behind his chair quoted Shakespeare: "The course of true love never did run true." Was President Gill a kindred spirit? Suddenly, the chair no longer felt so encompassing, the room so intimidating.

His eyes had followed mine to the poster. "Your degree in English Literature and your police experience, especially creating that juvenile outreach program, is the well-rounded background I want."

Nothing else about the interview came to mind as my dinner finally slogged its way to my gut, letting me breathe freely and dress for my overnight shift. Perhaps Anthony's expensive and militaristic proposals to solve security problems were why his hopes for the job had been quashed. Still, the atmosphere in my office over the past few weeks was that tonight was a Big Deal.

I left for campus at 10:30 p.m. wearing civilian clothes, a cap low over my forehead, and the walkie talkie hitched to my belt. So far, no reports of mischief had come in. The full moon lit my path as I cut across the town golf course, and the irony of whistling in appreciation stopped me short. A night of mischief, enhanced by that Blue Moon, lay ahead.

A T THE MAIN ROAD, a driver had just righted his overturned manure truck. I tamped down my twitchy nose at the smell, reported to dispatch, and grabbed a shovel.

Shortly after, Officer Perkins drove up in one of our two Cushman Carts. These lightweight electric utility vehicles cut through campus quickly and didn't damage grass and fields. I set my walkie talkie on the seat and resumed shoveling. Within an hour, the four of us had the road cleared. A local police patrol arrived as we finished. They ticketed the driver and thanked us for our help, holding their noses as they spoke, then turned and drove back into town. The manure truck driver waved and took off, leaving Perkins and me alone on the main road, stinking of manure.

"Well, chief, haven't seen that one before," said Perkins.

"Wha'da ya mean?"

"Think that wasn't a prank to distract us from campus?" She scratched her head and placed her cap back on. "This is what happens. Every year we set up a plan and something gets in the way."

The soft whirr of an electric engine wasn't enough warning before two laughing figures drove past in Perkin's Cushman. Costumed as a cobweb and a moth, they gave us a mock salute and drove across the golf course. Perkins and I chased on foot. She grabbed my arm and pointed off to the side. Our other Cushman, coming from campus, veered off the road onto the golf course. Trailing farther behind with each step was Officer Anthony. Had he run all the way from campus?

The second Cushman went up a small rise and down into the shallow frog pond that recent rain had deepened. The Cushman stalled and tipped over as the students jumped out. Anthony started down toward the pond, arms flailing giant windmill shadows on the moonlit grass as he slid, slipped, and fell in. The students ran after Perkins' Cushman, soggy costumes dragging along the ground behind them. Anthony rose, fist in the air, shouting at their backs as the Cushman and students were swallowed in a copse of trees.

Frustration warred with my ability to see the humor in the prank. Perkins smirked as Anthony trudged toward us. I sent him home to change while Perkins and I walked to campus.

——— ⟨∾⟩ ———

W E ARRIVED AT Campus Security where Beth was answering calls and dispatching patrols, wisps of hair falling out of her bun that held three pencils. She was sending lone officers to take reports and let the teams respond to new alerts.

Perkins took over while Beth updated me. Calls had multiplied as the students took advantage of the walkie-talkie I'd left in the Cushman. She had sent maintenance to Lysander Hall, the small dorm set up for students who preferred studies to parties, after several students reported someone had glued the keyholes to their rooms. While we spoke, a call came in that the larger dorm, Goodfellow Hall, had no water or lights. How could a dozen students cause such chaos?

Beth resumed her duties, and I sent Perkins and another guard to check out Goodfellow. Perkins called back and said the dorm was in chaos. Students had returned from a party to discover the water was shut off, lights were out, and all the communal bathroom faucet handles had been removed and laid in neat piles in one corner of each bathroom. "And," Perkins said, "students from the upper floors say their room keys don't work."

"OK. Be right over. Maintenance is still busy in Lysander. Find the electrical panel and get the lights back on. Then start fixing the faucets."

Six students met me at the Goodfellow entrance. The lights went on as I stepped inside. We took the elevator to five and tried one room, then another. No luck. Two students from the fourth floor left to try their rooms. I headed for the stairs, with one student joining me.

I stopped short in the stairwell and looked up a flight of stairs. "What the heck? I thought this dorm only had five floors."

"That's right." The student looked as perplexed as I felt. "Those shouldn't be there."

"No roof access from this stairwell?"

"Nope. Only from the east side of the building."

We walked up to the top floor and ran into the students who'd taken the elevator. According to the stairwell signs and room numbers, this was the fourth floor.

I rubbed my chin and said, "We've been pranked. It must have taken a bit of time to rewire the elevator and swap all the signs between these two floors. None of you saw anyone tampering with room signs or the elevator before you left?" A chorus of "No" and "Uh uh" left me clueless. I pulled out my notepad and starting writing. "What bar did you say you were at tonight?"

I T STAYED BUSY like that until dawn, when "The Star-Spangled Banner" blared over the sound system in the quad. I rushed across the street, past the library, and stopped. President Gill stood on the grass ahead, back to me, facing the administration building.

My throat dried. Parked across the landing at the top of the stairs were Gill's car, a wagon full of cows, and the two Cushman carts, their amber security lights flashing. Leading the lineup was a life-size, cardboard cutout of Officer Anthony rising from the frog pond, fist raised like Rambo, his mouth open in a giant snarl. Someone had placed a hockey puck in the cutout's raised fist. As the anthem neared its finale, fireworks lit the sky and awakened the dorm students and other neighbors.

Gill turned and removed his hand from his heart as I approached. *What must he think of me?*

Eyes twinkling, he said, "'Morning, Chief. In case you're wondering, I heard through the grapevine that someone *intimated* your job is on the line based on your performance tonight."

My jaw dropped, and he chuckled. "Not to worry. I meant it when I said we needed someone with your background."

He looked me in the eye. "April Fool's comes only once a year, and even Shakespeare had his mischief with *A Midsummer Night's Dream*."

Before I could respond, he turned back to the scene and pointed to Anthony's cardboard image. "Those who hobgoblin call you, and sweet Puck, you do their work, and they shall have good luck."

Ah, yes, Gill was a kindred spirit and, apparently, so were a few of these students.

Onta, Tell Me A Story

LIKONI PULLED THE BLANKET up to her chin and lay back in the bed. "Tell me a story, Onta. Tell me about the time the little people in the lowlands met our kind." She squirmed until her back found the right grooves. "I like that one."

Onta dimmed the light and pulled up a chair next to her. "That is a long story, and I still have work to do this night. I will tell you only part of it." The chair groan under her bulk as she sat, closed her eyes, and spoke in a soft, rhythmic cadence ...

————— ✥ —————

L ONG, LONG AGO, after the Great Disturbance had settled and the mountains no longer spewed liquid fire, the seas settled into place, one bordering east, another west. Our people had remained safe in these high mountains, for our shamans had kept the fires beneath our land calm. It took all our effort and aged some of the elders, who passed on their knowledge and slipped away to become one with the land.

In the lowlands, a high mountain range formed on the southern edge from the eastern sea to the center, where it met the Choch-Ha-ko-ee River and the great chasm. Beyond the chasm was the Dark Forest, so thick with trees and wildlife our kind did not explore it for we would not survive long in that hot, wet climate. The forest's expanse ran to the western sea, whose warm waters held strange fish that did not live in the cold eastern sea.

To go farther west from the Choch-ka-ho-ee, one had to travel north, beyond a mountain range smaller than ours but high enough to cut off the Dark Forest from the land north of it. To this day, the snow and water from that mountain runs south to the forest side, leaving the north a thirsty desert, where water hides beneath the ground, safe from the scorching sun. In some places, water bubbles to the surface and forms large, warm pools that support trees, plants, and animals. Outside those oases, only plants and animals able to live without water for many days can survive.

"Will our land ever become a desert, Mother?" Likoni's eyes were wide, even though she asked that question with each telling of the story.

"Not in our lifetime, little one. Our shamans will protect us."

Likoni sat up. "When do we get to Nanoni's story?"

Onta half-smiled and half-frowned until Likoni rolled her eyes and lay back down.

Onta closed her eyes. "Now, little daughter, comes the story of Nanoni and shish-Ka-toomi."

Nanoni and shish-Ka-toomi

NANONI WAS A LONELY child with a golden voice. Her family lived in the desert near the One Spring at the edge of the mountain. Many nights she lay awake, listening to the faint sounds of a flute coming from the mountain. In the light of day, shook their heads and muttered when she asked if they, too, heard it.

She became fascinated with the mountain, the flute, and the One Spring. The elders warned all the children to go there only with an elder, and even they did not approach it at night. Wolves lived near the mountain. And even the wolves slunk away when a Greoli appeared. This ferocious, long-toothed creature's head was haloed with wild blond hair. It had a long, lithe body and four enormous paws with sharp claws to stab into stone as it climbed, and its whipsaw tail could swat enemies across the water. If a Greoli drank from the water while you were there, you would turn into stone and the Greoli would trample your body until it was one with the dirt. So the elders said.

Nanoni wasn't afraid of wild beasts, not even a Greoli even though she nor anyone she'd asked had ever seen one. She could look any animal in the eye and it would obey, especially if she sang—although in truth, she had only done so with the village animals.

"My child, you would not see the Greoli," the others said when asked, "and thus not be able to look it in the eye. It need only lap water from the other side and you would turn to stone. Do not go near the One Spring alone or at night."

Young Nanoni, a free spirit, argued with the elders. "How do you know this, if they are ground into stone?"

"They never return. Where else would they be?"

Indeed, where had they gone? Where was her mother's mother, she who had disappeared when Nanoni was about five and her little sister was not yet born? And so many others before that?

No one other than Nanoni seemed interested in knowing. She would sneak off to the base of the mountain and play by herself among the boulders near the One Spring, hiding when villagers came for water. Perhaps she could spot a Greoli or find her missing greatmother. She would then say, "See, she was not stomped to stone by the Greoli. I have found her."

One day, while her parents hunted for food and her sister played with others, Nanoni went alone to the One Spring to draw water. As she knelt, ripples crossed the pond, and she looked up into the narrow, green eyes of a Greoli. The two stared at each other from across the water, Nanoni rising slowly with her eyes steady on the beast's.

The Greoli's fur bristled. It bared its teeth. Drool escaped from its mouth along with a low growl. Nanoni and the beast circled the spring, keeping the distance between them the same. She began to sing, weaving a song of enrapture that floated across the water and calmed the Greoli. It lay down and closed its eyes.

Nanoni continued singing while moving ever closer and ended her song when she finally stood beside it. The beast looked up, but instead of eating her, licked her hand. She giggled. It licked her hand again. And so, little by little, Nanoni learned that the beast wanted to hear her voice. She spoke, and it sighed. She sat next to it and sang. It snuggled up to her and placed its bear-sized head in her lap.

The day began to close, the sun moving closer to the ground. Still Nanoni sang. She stroked its fur and it rolled to its side, a sloppy, lopsided grin on its face. Nanoni knew her family would begin to search for her and feared what might happen if they came to the One Spring and saw the Greoli.

She said, "You must leave. My people will come and may hurt you if they find you here."

"Why would they hurt me, Nanoni?" said the beast.

Nanoni gasped. "You speak!"

"Only in your mind. And in your mind only." The beast sat up, towering over her as she was still seated. "Go now. Return to your people. Do not speak of me, for they will not understand. When the night is full and the moon begins to steal away, return here. I will tell you more."

"May I know your name, great beast? And how will I know you from your kind?"

"Do not worry. My kind will know you and that you befriended me. None will harm you, for I, shish-Ka-toomi, have declared you friend."

Nanoni gave shish-Ka-toomi a hug, picked up her bucket, which was now strangely full, and returned to her desert village. Everyone was angry with her for giving them a fright. She said nothing about the great beast and took her water bucket into her family hut.

Late that night, Nanoni slipped out of the bed she shared with her younger sister and grabbed the cloak she'd stuffed underneath earlier. She tiptoed past her parents' sleeping room and out the door that gave no sound, for she'd greased its hinges with animal fat after dinner that evening. Once outside, she put on her shoes, bundled her cloak around her against the night chill, and ran across the desert to the One Spring.

shish-Ka-toomi was waiting for her. She rushed over in greeting when out from behind him appeared a Greoli pup. She cried out in joy and bent over to hug it when shish-Ka-toomi pushed her back with his giant paw. "He is injured. He needs your help."

Nanoni examined the pup in the moonlight. One leg dangled without firmness, and the pup could put no weight on it. She sat on the ground and let the pup crawl into her lap. Singing softly, she examined the injured leg, ran her gentle fingers up and down its length, avoiding the most swollen area near the paw. "It is broken, shish-Ka-toomi."

"Can you fix it?"

"I can only try. I am not a healer, but I have helped the healer splint a little girl's leg so the bone could grow back together and she could walk again. It took a long time. And she now walks with a limp."

"That is better than not walking at all. Come to my den and make this splint to heal my son."

Nanoni picked up the cub and set it on shish-Ka-toomi's back. He led them toward the mountain. Nanoni stopped and said, "I am not permitted there."

"Your people fear what they do not know. But in you, I see great curiosity, truth, and trust. That is why I chose you. You want to know what is on the other side. And I need you to heal my son. Please. No harm will come to you."

Nanoni swallowed, clenched and unclenched her hands, then stepped forward. "Yes. I will come. I will help your son."

And so they trudged up the hill leading into the mountain and entered a cave so dark Nanoni had to hold onto the pup's fur for guidance. Tiny, winged insects led their way, throwing off sparkles of light as they flittered ahead. Nanoni began to see the outlines of the walls and ceiling. They entered a large cavern, the ceiling alive with the insects' light. Her footsteps echoed, and water trickled nearby. shish-Ka-toomi sat and crooned. Dozens of pairs of eyes opened in a semicircle around a small stream.

"This is my family, my clan. We are the Nanochkee. They know you are here to help and will not harm you." They stepped over the trickling stream of water and the air around her rippled. She had a sudden knowing that the stream fed the One Spring. She shivered in awe at the names and faces of missing villagers flowing through her mind—some gone so many years they were forgotten, including entire generations of her mother's family.

shish-Ka-toomi introduced her to each member of his clan. She could hardly keep the names straight except the one with the white streak down her snout: Toomi-oh, his mate. Their pup's name was shish-Ho-ra.

Toomi-oh led them out of the cavern and into a forest so dark the moon did not break through. This was their home, the cavern simply a barrier between the world of the Nanochkee and Nanoni's tribe. She followed the flittering lights, gathered several sticks, and cut lengths of vine with the knife she, like all villagers, carried.

She said, "I will have to pull on his paw, to make the bones line up properly. It will hurt and he will cry."

Toomi-oh said she would hold her son down and not let him bite. Nanoni sang a soothing song as she straightened shish-Ho-ra's leg and wrapped a crude splint around it. "He should not put weight on it until it heals."

When she finished, light was filtering through the trees and Nanoni saw a lone hut nearby. "Daylight comes. But if I return to my village, who will care for shish-Ho-ra?"

shish-Ka-toomi said, "Write a note to your people that you are safe. I will leave it by the spring so when they come for the day's water, they will find it. You know you will not see them again?"

Nanoni nodded, tore a scrap torn from her nightdress, and with the burnt end of a stick drew a scene of her hugging her parents and little sister and another of her walking away from the village.

What a wondrous place her new home was. She stepped into the hut and picked up the flute on the bed, knowing she was here to replace the last missing villager—her mother's mother—who had died of old age.

One day, I may return and speak of my adventures.

Most Likely to Succeed

RUPERT SHANES DESERVES a proper burial. Someone just has to kill him first.

Cici pushed the thought aside lest she blurt it out and, if something happened to Rupert, she'd be suspected. Deep breath, check the rearview. *Okay, makeup hides the slap marks on my face.*

The car radio blared AC/DC's oldie hit, "Dirty Deeds Done Dirt Cheap," reminding her she'd never escape Rupert's reach. She punched the off button. *Won't anyone put that man out of our misery?*

When she reached the diner, Cici plumped her hair, moistened her lips with her tongue, and went inside, ready to face her old gang from high school.

SITTING ALONE IN the diner, Roberta "call me Berta" ordered a coffee refill and examined the menu. Same luncheon specials as twenty-five years ago. She hated the nickname she'd earned in high school. But *Flirta Berta* fit, even now. After graduation she'd sought stardom and love far from this sleepy New England valley. Stardom had eluded her. Love ... well, that was tricky.

Ex number one was a cheat. When he objected to a divorce, she slapped their prenup on the table and walked away from the marriage with a mortgage-free house and the weighty diamond that sparkled on her right ring finger. Her second husband had been a treasure. She'd not flirted once after he'd proposed. Their marriage was good until his accidental death four years ago fractured her bliss. Then she buried herself in her job at an L.A. ad agency.

Cici waved from the doorway and joined her at their long-ago usual table. They hugged and air kissed, Cici's shiny blond bob in stark contrast to Berta's bottle-brilliant red locks that matched her manicured nails.

T ERRY VIEWED THE frayed collar on his one clean button-down shirt and grabbed a turtleneck from his suitcase. Late. *Oh well, let them think I'm too busy with work to be on time. They don't need to know I'm unemployed ... again.*

His open yearbook displayed his younger self—title-winning quarterback sporting a triumphant grin, football raised in the air, helmet under the other arm. Terry in the mirror? Time and gravity had delivered his chest south. Food and drink had expanded the photo's trim waistline that now drooped over his belt. He applied brown hair coloring to what was left of his hair. *Should I even go?*

The yearbook page flipped over, revealing a photo of Valerie, his senior prom date. *I can't live like this any longer. It has to end.* He slammed the yearbook shut, plunked a newsboy cap on his head, and left the motel.

DAN ARRIVED AT the diner and hustled to their old table, tossing his newspaper down as he greeted them. The headline announced the House of Representatives' impeachment inquiry into President Clinton. Dan ran a hand through his hair and slid into the booth next to Berta. His crush on her was long over, but he enjoyed her warm hip sidling up to his. He looked at his watch. "Where's Terry? He should be here by now."

"Terry's never on time." Cici pushed the newspaper aside and picked up the menu. "Let's order. If we wait for him, we'll have to get it to go."

Berta asked Dan how he could get away on a weekday.

"My daughter's been apprenticing to learn the business. She can handle things for a few days. How about you?"

She waved a hand in the air. "I went to L.A. to be a star. Didn't happen. Now? Manage a creative team at an ad agency. Turns out I'm good at it. I took vacation time so I can hike in the gorge and revel in the smell of a New England fall."

They spent the next twenty minutes comparing their high school dreams to the lives they now led.

———— ⚬ ————

TERRY PARKED A block away to conceal the beater he drove. He sucked in his gut to pump up his chest and hide his girth as he walked to the diner. Out of breath, he opened the door as the waitress was setting plates on their old table. He slapped Dan on the back and mumbled about a work emergency. He leaned over to buss Berta's cheek and slid in next to Cici, kissing her cheek. "Cecily, we're next to each other as usual."

"Really, Terry? Since when have I been called Cecily?"

She resumed her conversation about the new high school. "So, we're the first reunion in it. Pretty neat, huh?"

Terry's face flushed at Cici's rebuff. She'd never spoken to him like that before. He ordered the luncheon special without looking at the menu. His life on the road, through small towns and large cities, had taught him to go with a diner's special; it was usually the most edible and cheapest meal of his day.

— ⟨◦⟩ —

SMALL TALK PUNCTUATED with bursts of laughter over suddenly-remembered incidents lengthened their lunch. Terry's exploits on the field, Dan's science experiments that sometimes ended badly, Berta's leading roles in the school plays with Cici supporting—they made it sound more fun than some of it had been.

Berta invited them to her hotel. "With so many classmates in town for the reunion, I ordered a suite to entertain. You can help me break it in."

Cici offered to pick up snacks. Dan said he'd hit the *packie* for beer and wine. "Should I get anything else, Berta? Maybe vodka, scotch, soda?"

"Sure honey, that sounds great. I'll go ahead and tidy up. Give me a half hour. Suite 780." She winked at Dan as he let her out of the booth.

— ⟨◦⟩ —

DRINKS FLOWED IN Berta's suite. The conversation turned from reminiscence to what they'd been up to since graduation. Dan and Cici had remained in the valley and in touch with each other. Berta and Cici had connected by email occasionally over the years. Terry hadn't been in touch with any of them until the reunion mail caught up with him. He spoke of a traveling sales job and lousy bosses who ignored his business advice because he didn't have a degree.

"Say, whatever happened to that football scholarship you had to State?" Dan, relaxing in an easy chair, knew the answer but wanted to see what Terry would say.

"Oh, that. Well, I blew out my shoulder in the first year." Terry, seated on one couch, flexed his arm as if it pained him. "Couldn't throw the long ball anymore, lost the scholarship. No more school."

"I'm sorry" and "too bad" came from Cici and Berta, sitting on the couch opposite Terry. Dan said nothing. He had learned the truth when he'd joined the board of the college; Terry was thrown out for cheating and excessive drinking.

Berta turned on lamps as the sun dropped. "Whatever happened to Rupert Shanes, *Mr. Most Likely to Succeed?* He was supposed to make it big in business or politics. I thought he'd be, like, a Warren Buffet or something."

Cici shuddered at Berta's question. Dan cleared his throat and said, "Rupert turned his father's tiny, used-car lot into the largest dealership in the Tri-Valley. Has his hand in a few other businesses, too."

Berta said, "That's it? Mr. Blond Bombshell seemed destined to own the whole valley."

"Well, his name isn't on any legal papers ..." Dan said.

"Ooh, do tell. This sounds interesting." Berta glanced at her nails and sat again.

Dan refilled his drink. "Rupert's a loan shark. Everyone knows. Nobody does anything. He's a nasty, lying piece of crap. I wish he'd been in that car crash after the prom, instead of Valerie." He sighed, leaned back, and put the glass to his forehead, as if the ice could melt the memories.

Terry almost dropped his glass.

Berta said, "Wow. I'm sorry I even mentioned Rupert."

"No harm. How could you know?" said Cici. "He's getting an award. *Mr. Most Likely* who actually lived up to his potential. I don't know who came up with that idea."

Dan said, "He's worse now. It started in high school, maybe junior high. I kicked his butt once, after he'd victimized one of my buddies in the Science Club. Thought it'd straighten him out. Instead, he got better at protecting himself."

Cici said, "With Rupert it's all hustle ... and muscle when you can't pay him back." She pulled her pashmina scarf closer around her shoulders. "He'll be there this weekend, looking out for his *interests*." She used her fingers to mark air quotes around the word interests.

Terry's eyes narrowed as he looked at Cici and swirled the ice in his soda glass. His husky voice quivered. "I thought I was the only one he tortured."

Dan leaned forward. "What?"

Terry stared at his feet, capped head hunched between his shoulders. "I've lied to you ... to everyone. I'm unemployed, have no friends. Rupert's ... blackmailing me. Cost me my wife, house, jobs ... everything."

He looked up, tears threatening to spill. "Every time I start to piece my life back together, he's there, wanting more. I change cities and somehow he finds me. I came to the reunion to have it out with him."

"All these years? What could you have done ...?" Berta said.

Hands shaking, he set his glass on the table. "I ... I killed Valerie ... in that crash." Tears escaped. "Then I ran like the coward I am."

Dan frowned. "That can't be right." He got up and paced the room. "Look, what does everyone remember from prom night, after we got to the party?"

Cici leaned back and tented her fingers, eyes unfocused, then said, "It was swinging when me, Berta, and our dates got there. The guys went for food and drink, probably looking for the spiked punch. Berta and I stayed on the porch."

Berta said, "Terry, you were already *plastered*."

Cici nodded. "Val was furious. She took your keys."

Terry jerked his head up. "What? But I was driving ... the car she was killed in." His eyes darted to each friend.

"Uh uh. She was driving ..." Berta said. "Wasn't she?"

He blinked. "I wasn't with her?" His mouth opened again but no words came out.

Dan looked down at Terry. "Why do you think you were driving?"

"Rupert said I was." His voice became soft, childlike. "I'd borrowed a junker from his dad's lot. I remember a chugging contest. Next thing I knew, I was standing beside a tree. The car was all smashed into it with Val in the passenger seat. I just knew she was dead.

"Then Rupert was there. Said he was out walking and saw me get out of the driver's seat after the crash. He positioned Val behind the wheel to make it look like she was driving. We heard sirens and ran. Rupert took off in another direction after we got near the main road." Terry held his head in both hands.

Dan sat beside him. "You weren't driving, Terry. You weren't even in the car."

Terry stared at Dan. "How ... how could you know that?"

"You made a scene after Valerie took your keys. I drove you around to calm you down. You said you wanted to walk it off. I let you out near the pond and you headed into the woods. You would have come out right near crash site. Terry, you couldn't have been in the car with Val."

"All these years ... Rupert's made me believe I'd killed her."

Berta said, "I saw Val get in the passenger side of that old heap. Later, I assumed she'd slid over to drive herself home."

Cici said, "Terry, Rupert was drinking, too, but not as much as you. I bet he crashed the car, saw you, and set you up."

"That would be just like him." Dan stood up to refresh his drink, reached past the hard liquor, and poured a soda. "All this talk of drunken accidents ..."

Cici sat next to Terry and laid her hand on his knee. "Rupert must be stopped. I ... I wasn't going to tell anyone else this. Dan already knows."

Her fingers whitened where she clutched her glass. "I worked for him, years ago. I 'borrowed' from the work account to pay for my mom's medical care. She died anyway. I worked an extra job to sneak the money back before our audit. Somehow, Rupert found out. He made me sleep with him as 'final payment.' Only with him, it's never final." She downed her drink in one gulp. "He takes me whenever he wants. But hearing this, Terry? I hate him even more."

Berta plunked her drink on the coffee table. "Well, we've got two days. Let's put this suite to good use and figure a way to teach Rupert Shanes a lesson."

———— ⚬⚬⚬ ————

THE FOUR REGROUPED in Berta's suite the next morning. Over breakfast, Dan revealed more about Rupert. "His car business is the only legitimate thing about him. He hires top people for good pay and doesn't cheat on things related to the dealership. Doesn't have to. He gets tons of financial details through car loans and has a private detective on payroll. That gives him plenty of victims for loan-sharking and blackmail. Lately, he's been running investment schemes on retirees."

"No kidding." Cici twirled a finger around the tassel on her scarf. "Just when they're most vulnerable."

Terry slumped further into the sofa. "So, he keeps finding me through that detective? You can't beat someone like that."

"We can," Dan said, "if we plan carefully. Everyone here, except maybe you Berta, has good reason to try."

"Oh, I'm in, honey. That man was nasty then, and he's for sure worse now. What's your reason?"

"My business partner ... my best friend, put a gun to his head because of Rupert. Since then, his brother Greg and I have been collecting evidence and sharing it with their sister. She's a state police detective."

Terry looked up. "What're they doing?"

"Investigating, but solid proof is hard to get, and Rupert has to be taken down by authorities outside the valley."

"Why outside the valley?"

"His debtors include politicians, law enforcement, any suffering souls who'll repay with leads on who's sleeping around, got elderly parents with huge medical bills, or has a gambling itch. We know it, just can't prove it ... yet."

Berta said, "Cici and I had some ideas last —"

A knock on the door interrupted her. Dan stood. "That'll be Greg's sister. I invited her." He went to the door with Berta, and they ushered in a striking thirties-something woman followed by an older man and woman, all dressed in street clothes.

"I'm Sara. Dan asked me to meet you. I brought two others from my investigation team."

After introductions, Berta picked up where she'd left off. "Cici and I talked about setting Rupert up at the Saturday night reunion dinner. We'd need someone looking for an investment opportunity."

She pointed at Sara. "You'd be perfect as Val, a classmate Rupert can't remember with the same name as someone we think he killed. These other two," she pointed again, "could be a couple looking for retirement investment opportunities."

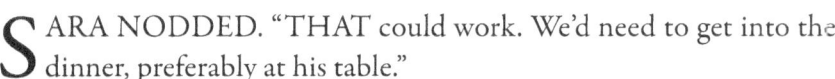

SARA NODDED. "THAT could work. We'd need to get into the dinner, preferably at his table."

Cici called the reunion organizer, a trusted friend. "Can you seat three more at Rupert Shanes' table? They really want to meet him." She listened. "That's great. Remember, this is just between us. See you Saturday."

She turned to the group. "She's happy to add you three. Seems like a few people started playing shuffle-seat to get away from Rupert's table once the assignments were released."

Berta retrieved her jewelry from the safe and set it on the coffee table. Sorting through it took only a few minutes, and she distributed several pieces to the three detectives. "Wear these. You'll scream money to Rupert if he knows anything about jewelry."

Terry asked, "What should I do?"

Cici touched his arm. "You've spent twenty-five years paying for something you didn't do. That's more than enough."

Sara said. "You're still in trouble for withholding information in that crash."

"I don't care. As long as Rupert pays for what he's done."

She nodded. "Okay. You'll have one of the biggest parts in this ... getting us into Rupert's office."

B RILLIANT RED, YELLOW, and purple leaves contrasted against the darkening sky as two cars pulled into the partially-filled parking lot for Valley High's Class of 1973 twenty-fifth reunion. Dan drove Berta. Terry rode with Cici, grateful no one would see his clunker. He swept his hand through the sprinkles of white in his sparse hair.

"Stop that, Terry. Get over it. None of us is a kid anymore."

"Jeezer, you were never this sharp or grumpy in high school."

"Sorry. Nerves, I guess. At the diner, I felt like you still hadn't grown up. We're all older. We change."

"Not Rupert Shanes."

"No," she agreed, "not Rupert Shanes."

In the final moments of the sun slipping behind the trees, they smoothed their suits and dresses, avoiding the microphones taped to their skin. Terry pulled in a deep breath, the dying autumn leaves triggering the memory of warm apple pie with vanilla ice cream melting on top. And football seasons past. He wriggled his shoulders, straightened his tie, and took Cici's arm, following Dan and Berta through the fallen leaves splayed across the parking lot.

The four signed in and attached name badges to their chests. Rupert stood off to the far side of the ballroom speaking with someone who frowned and shook his head. Rupert's black designer suit, shirt, and tie, and blond hair slicked back from the front, oozed charm that belied the snake beneath. Cici and Terry both stepped back, Cici bumping into Dan.

She poked Berta. "Looks like he's got another fish on the line."

Dan looked between Cici and Terry's shoulders and said, "Billy Temple. Gambling problem. Heard he's into Rupert big. I'll try to pull him away. Might get more info to use."

"Let me, Dan," Berta said. "This calls for a bit of acting."

Berta strolled away, waving at the two men, and took Billy's arm. Hands in his pockets, Rupert scowled as she flipped a comment to him over her shoulder and escorted Billy to the bar on the far side of the room.

Cici checked Terry's name badge. "We're looking for table fifteen. It's on that side, nowhere near Rupert's."

Terry sucked in his gut and smiled, shook hands, and clapped backs until he reached table fifteen, where he dropped into the chair like a flat tire. *Whew. Gonna be a long night.*

Cici and Dan chit chatted and agreed to table-hop later as they wound their way through the room, joining Terry minutes later. By now, the room was almost full, the line at the bar had grown, and the DJ was playing music from the seventies.

Dan slipped into the drink line with Berta and Billy, pumped Billy's hand, and pointed to table fifteen while speaking. Billy looked skeptical. Berta slipped her hand around his arm and whispered in his ear. He nodded as they reached the bartender.

R UPERT WATCHED BERTA and Billy walk away. A sour taste rose in his throat as he moved toward the nearby bar for a fresh drink. What could Berta want with loser Billy? That rock on her finger and the necklace around her plump neck seem genuine. If her expensive tastes are matched by income—

A woman he didn't recognize grabbed his arm. "Hello, Rupert. Looks like you're here solo, too. And look," she pointed at his name tag, "we're seated at the same table."

"Sorry, don't recognize you ..." Rupert prided himself on never forgetting a face; it was central to his business. He looked at the name tag. Valerie, no last name. "You went to Valley High?"

He swallowed. Who is this woman? I don't remember another Valerie in my class.

"Oh, yes. Time of my life, although I was a wallflower back then. It's hard to come to one of these things alone, so I brought friends." She introduced him to the older couple with her. They looked well off, right down to what looked like genuine rubies in the woman's necklace and earrings. He began to excuse himself but the two women each took an arm and escorted him to his table, the man following. Oh, well. Maybe he'd learn something that would lead to more business deals—the kind he liked to hold after hours.

Val said her friends were retiring from the military, had money saved, and wanted to settle in the valley. Did he know of any business opportunities they could buy into? He shrugged noncommittally. This woman was no wallflower, and he usually initiated business talks. She pressed. His vague response was drowned out as other couples joined the table, introductions were repeated, and the music grew louder. He relaxed and engaged in small talk with others at the table.

Terry dropped by, smiled broadly at Val, and said something about a class they were in together. Confused, Rupert still couldn't place her as a classmate.

Terry nodded curtly to Rupert, "I understand congratulations are in order. You're getting some sort of award?"

Rupert nodded as he chewed on an hors d'oeuvre.

Terry said to the group. "Hope you don't mind if I pull Rupert away for a minute."

He took Rupert's elbow and guided him to a corner of the room. "Look. I can't do this anymore. I came here tonight to tell you I'm done paying you."

"Are you crazy? You want to go to jail?" Rupert jerked his chin toward the table they'd just left. "And who is that woman, Val? I don't remember her."

"You wouldn't. She didn't hang with vermin." Terry moved closer and lowered his voice. "I finally figured something out. If you knew I'd been driving Val that night, and you covered it up all these years, legally you're just as guilty. Even if I go to jail, I'll have the satisfaction of knowing you'll be there, too."

"What? You suddenly grow a pair?" Rupert's eyes darted around the crowded room. "We can't talk about this here."

"Fine. Tomorrow. Your office."

Rupert poked his finger into Terry's chest. "Six a.m. Don't be late."

Rupert refreshed his drink at the bar and returned to the table. *Time to see if I can charm my way into a business deal with this new couple. They seem eager. I doubt their military background has taught them anything about business. I'll have my guy check them out on Monday.*

P ROMPTLY AT SIX the next morning, Rupert answered the knock on his private rear door to admit Terry. Rupert raised his eyebrows at Cici's presence, but ushered both in, his back to them when she smushed a wad of gum against the door's strike plate. He sat behind his desk and motioned to the stiff chairs in front of it.

Terry sat in one. Cici sat on the couch beneath the window. "I don't need an interrogation chair. I prefer to be comfortable."

"Suit yourself, although I don't understand why you're here. If Terry knew—"

"He knows."

"Then why are you here?"

"I want my mother's ring back. You know. The one I saw you ogling the first time you forced yourself on me in my home. It was missing afterward."

Rupert chuckled and leaned back in the chair until it bumped against the safe behind him. "What makes you think I'd give it back? Anyway, I'm here to talk with Terry."

"Yes. About prom night. About him driving the car that killed Valerie." She leaned forward, eyes sparkling. "Except now he knows YOU were driving that car."

Rupert bolted upright in the chair, his waist bumping the edge of the desk. "What did you say?"

"We know you drove off from the party with Val. Terry was out walking. You tricked him."

"Yeah, but you can't prove it. As for your mother's ring, you can have it. Turns out it isn't worth anything." He turned to the safe, dialed the code, and opened the door. He grabbed an envelope and pointed it toward Cici.

"You stole it. You bring it to me."

"Oh for cryin' out loud. You two are pathetic." He walked over to Cici and dropped the envelope past her outstretched hand into her lap.

The rear door burst open, and three state troopers rushed in. One held the safe door open, another grappled with Rupert, and the third blocked the door to the dealership showroom.

Handcuffed, Rupert jerked away. "What is this? How did you get in here?" His face reddened as looked at the trooper's face. "Aren't you ... Val, from last night?" His face paled and reddened again as he recognized the other two troopers. He slumped into the chair next to Terry, who rose and moved to the couch with Cici.

Terry said, "I can see his red, debtors' ledger from here. Under that pile of papers. There's your evidence."

Sara said, "Plain sight. Take it out."

Rupert shouted that they had no right to do this. She told him to shut up. One trooper looked through the ledger and confirmed that it contained payoffs from dozens, including politicians and law officers. The other began bagging everything in the safe as evidence while Sara arrested Rupert and removed him from the scene.

———— ⊙∾⊙ ————

TESTIMONY FROM CICI, Berta, Dan, and Terry, along with the account book detailing the usury against Terry, Billy, and others, was a main feature in the indictments against Rupert and his associates. The *Tri-Valley News* ran front-page articles for days as reporters gleaned new facts from the arrests and arraignments of so many prominent valley members.

Rupert's tentacles had extended throughout and beyond the Tri-Valley. Weeks and even months later, new articles appeared on inside pages as the investigation expanded and progressed. The state police arrested several high-ranking officers of the local police department, four town aldermen, and three city councilors, leading to suspensions and resignations. Similar arrests occurred in half a dozen other towns.

Berta extended her vacation and stayed with Cici to help Terry through his legal defense of hiding the truth about the car crash. He was found guilty of withholding evidence in Valerie's manslaughter. In sentencing him, the judge declared that he had served his sentence under Rupert's blackmail.

Berta returned for the trials and stayed, retiring from her job and selling her LA home. The four friends were reviled by many—those who now had to pay for their crimes. Others were so grateful to be out from under Rupert's grasp that they pled guilty and served small bits of time in jail, performed community service, or were on probation.

Rupert's own words on reunion night and in his office Sunday morning frosted the cake the four friends had served. He was convicted and given the maximum sentence.

T HE FOUR WALKED to the diner after Rupert's sentencing, sitting in the same seats as their first day before the reunion. Berta asked Terry his plans.

"I don't know. I can't stay in Cici's garage apartment forever. Guess it's time to move on." His eyes drifted to the menu in front of him.

Dan cleared his throat and said, "Look. I understand, now, why you were so mixed up in college. The strain you were under then and have lived with for so long since. Rupert broke my partner. He didn't break you."

"He almost did." Terry choked on his words and grabbed the water glass but didn't raise it off the table.

Dan reached across the table and tapped the back of Terry's hand. "I judged you harshly without knowing the whole story. Let me make it up to you. Come work for me, show what you can do when you're not running from the past."

Cici raised her glass. "Say yes, Terry. You can stay in that apartment until you've got your finances in better shape, even pay rent if it makes you feel better. The four of us make a good team. Let's promise to be there for each other from now on."

The waitress returned to take their order, but they were headed out the door. A ten- dollar bill on the table was accompanied by a note on the napkin:

"Changed our minds — headed for a celebration lunch with drinks. Dan"

The Pixie Path Home

EIGHT-YEAR-OLD CHLOE McFarland followed her brother Paul, who dragged an empty sled between them up the steep hill. Weighted with heavy boots, pants, and coat, her short legs could not match Paul's stride. While the sled slid harmlessly across the frozen crust atop the six inches of yesterday's snowfall, her feet punctured through with every step.

"Paul, slow down. I can't keep up." She wiped her nose with a handkerchief and stuffed it back into her coat pocket.

He turned around. "Hurry up, Chloe. We gotta finish before Mrs. Adams wakes up from her nap and sees we're gone." Two years older and four or five inches taller than Chloe, he had the advantage in the deep snow.

"My legs are shorter than yours." Chloe imagined that the puffy clouds following each word curled like the smoke from father's pipe. She sighed and started uphill again.

Paul stretched out his hand and helped her up the last few steps to the crest. "Look how small everything is from here."

"Are you sure we won't get into trouble? Mother doesn't like us going into the woods without a grown-up." Chloe looked down the hill.

Their two-story home lay directly below and faced the village square. Smoke rose from every chimney of the dozen or more houses at the base of the hillside. They lay in a horseshoe shape around a field in the center where the village held celebrations and children played. Several snow figures dotted the field, but no children were out in today's bitter cold. A road followed the U-shape, dividing the houses from the square. A horse-drawn carriage clipped along the road, heading out of the village. The seamstress and a young girl exited a carriage that was stopped in front of the seamstress' home.

"Look, Paul. That must be Mrs. Schneider with her granddaughter. Now I won't be the new girl in school."

"What's so bad about being new? You made friends pretty fast."

Chloe sighed and scuffed her foot. He wouldn't understand. He'd met Fritz the day they'd arrived, and the two became friends right away. Her first week at school had been lonely and embarrassing. The teachers made her sit in the front of the room, as if she had to be supervised in order to behave. The girls in her class pointed at her red hair and giggled. Someone sneaked up behind her and pulled it, then ran off squealing, "It is real."

After another week, Betsy – or Elizabeth as the teachers called her – sat next to her on the stairs at recess and asked her to join in their game. She was accepted, but still the *new girl.*

Chloe turned to Paul, "I wonder how fast we'd go if we sledded from here?"

"Won't know until we try. But we got one thing to do first." He shifted the bulky pack on his back, grabbed the rope to the sled, and headed off-path into the woods.

Chloe glanced again at the scene below, then hurried after him. Her curls escaped from beneath her hat and danced across her face as the snow and heavy clothing forced her into a rocking gait.

The snow wasn't as deep once they ventured further into the forest, and Chloe kept pace with the sled. "Paul, we're not supposed to go this way. Father said it's not safe."

Paul stopped and faced her. The sled bumped against his shins. "He said *you* shouldn't. He never said it to me. It'll be all right as long as you're with me. I promise we'll stay on our property. I got it all mapped out here." He tapped his head with a mittened hand.

His frown said he wouldn't listen, so she shook her head and began walking again. He usually won their arguments. They didn't often get into trouble, but this felt like one of those times.

------ ⟡ ------

ABOUT TWENTY MINUTES later, Paul stopped and pointed to a six-foot fir at the outer edge of a cluster of young trees near a long downward slope into more dense forest. "There it is. The perfect Christmas Tree."

"That's why you put the wide runners on the sled." Chloe nodded at her brother's genius. He was clever with tools and making things while she was book smart.

Paul pulled a small axe out of his pack and began whacking at the base of the tree. Ten minutes later, he removed his heavy coat and pushed the sleeves of his knit sweater up to his elbows. "This is harder work than I thought. I should have sharpened the axe."

Chloe watched from her perch on the sled, absentmindedly eating snow she scooped from the ground. "I'm cold, Paul, and it smells like it's going to snow again. How much longer?"

"You wouldn't be cold if you were doing this. And if you're cold, stop eating snow." He shook his head and continued working.

After a few more whacks, he stopped again. "Almost done. Bring me a rope from my pack. I don't want this to fall the wrong way."

"Where'd you learn about chopping trees? We've always lived in the city—until now." Chloe rummaged in the pack, sneaked a small bundle that smelled like cinnamon cookies into her coat pocket, then handed the rope to Paul.

"Fritz showed me the other day. We cut one down for his grandmother. When I saw how happy it made her ... well, I came up here and found this one. I want to make mother happy."

He sniffled. Chloe wiped her eyes with her handkerchief and stuffed it in her pocket again. Christmas wouldn't be the same without Father.

Christopher McFarland was away on railroad business. He was an expert on the knuckle-coupler, the railroad's newest way to couple train cars together, and the automatic air brake system that made trains safer. But why did he have to go away so soon after moving to this new, bigger home in the country? Would he get home in time for Christmas?

"Chloe. Come help me with this." Paul had tied the rope around the trunk as high as he could reach. She untangled the loose end of the rope.

He dragged it to the biggest tree away from the edge of the slope, wrapped it twice around, and pulled it taut before tying a tight knot. "That should keep it from sliding down that slope. Better stand out of the way."

She waited behind another tree as Paul gave the final chops that severed his chosen tree from its base. He whooped when it fell away from the slope. The siblings wrestled the tree onto the sled. First, it slid off the other side. Then it rolled and turned sideways. They finally secured it with the rope Paul had attached earlier.

He tied a second, shorter rope to the trunk and handed it to her. "Make sure the back end stays straight behind me and doesn't bump into trees or fall off the sled. We don't want to do all that work twice."

She nodded, picked up the rope, studying the sled while he put on his coat and pack. "Paul, isn't the sled pointed in the wrong direction? How will we turn it around with the tree sticking off both ends?"

"Don't worry. I'll drag it closer to the edge where's there's some open space." He grabbed the lead rope and pulled, falling on his backside as the sled resisted. Their efforts to get the tree onto the sled had wedged it into the snow. He wrapped the rope around his forearm and pulled again.

Chloe pushed against the trunk. The sled pulled free. She fell forward as the tree slipped from her grasp. The tree knocked Paul aside and the sled rushed toward the slope, dragging him behind. Over the edge went the tree, the sled, and Paul.

Down to the place where the children were not allowed.

Chloe shivered. The girls at school said elves and pixies lived in that section of the forest. Grown-ups pooh-poohed that, but also said that place was dangerous and to stay away.

She ran to the edge of the slope and crouched. "Paul," she yelled, then held her breath. "Paul. Are you all right?"

The sled had left a fairly straight path, but Paul's zig-zag pattern on one side brushed against bushes and small trees. Had he crashed into any of them? She couldn't see into the thicket that had swallowed the sled and her brother.

"Help, I'm stuck." Paul's faint voice, at last.

Chloe sat and swung her legs around to the front and lifted her feet off the ground. Praying that pixies weren't real, she pushed herself over the edge and became a sled, shifting her weight to steer her body along the sled's path.

THE SLOPE LEVELED off into a shallow clearing, and Chloe slid to a stop. Ahead of her, lay Paul half-buried in snow. He was wedged between a tree and a boulder with his head raised above the pack like a turtle inspecting the world.

"Paul, are you hurt?" She brushed snow off her arms and legs as she trudged over to him.

"I'm all right. Just stuck. It's the pack, I think." Kneeling, she dug his legs free with her hands, shivering as the snow that had piled inside her jacket on her downhill slide trickled down her back and pants. She moved up to his back. The pack was holding him hostage.

She unbuckled the straps at the bottom of the pack. "Can you crawl out now?"

He inched his way forward, stood, and faced his sister. "Thanks. I don't know what I'd have done if you weren't here."

Chloe giggled and stood up. "You look like a snowman." She brushed snow off her legs and wriggled her shoulders as snow melted under her coat.

"Look in a mirror. You're pretty funny looking right now, too." He bent down and dislodged the pack, buckled the straps, and hoisted it on again.

She pulled clumps of ice off her woolen mittens and from her curls. "Paul, your face is bleeding."

He removed a mitten and felt his face. "Just scratches. I mostly protected my face with my arm."

"Why didn't you let go of the sled?"

He raised his other arm. Dangling from it was the broken end of the rope from the sled. He unraveled it and stuffed it in his coat pocket.

"Oh. At least the rope broke and not your arm."

"Let's get the tree back up the hill. We need to be home before dark."

"Paul, Mrs. Adams must be awake by now. She'll be frantic that we're gone."

"You're right. But what can we do? We have to get home."

"If we leave the tree here, maybe Fritz will come back with us tomorrow and help."

Paul stamped his foot. "No. It's a surprise. We need to take the tree home now so I can decorate it tonight."

Chloe frowned. There was that look again. She didn't want him to be mad at her, but it would be dark soon. That's when the forest was extra scary. Even if fairies and pixies weren't real, bears and other animals surely must wander here.

She reached into a pocket for her handkerchief. Wrong pocket. She removed the small bundle she'd taken from Paul's pack earlier and opened it. The cookies had broken into many pieces during her trip down the slope.

"Hey, that's mine. Fritz's mother gave them to me." Paul grabbed for her hand, but Chloe jerked it away. He tripped on a bush hidden under the snow and fell.

She put a few pieces of cookie into her mouth. The crumbles blended into the savory flavors of sugar, cinnamon, and raisin. Smacking her lips, she said, "You're wuppofed to fware."

Paul got up, frowned at his sister, and brushed himself off. Chloe extended the cookies toward him. He extracted a few large pieces before she closed the bundle and put it back in her pocket.

"We got to get the tree—"

A voice squeaked from behind them, "What have we here? Two little people lost in the woods, perhaps? Do I smell cookies, too?"

They whirled around, but there was only forest.

The voice came again, this time from their right. "I know the way out ... for a price."

They whirled again. No one there.

"Paul, I'm scared." Chloe retrieved her handkerchief and wiped her nose.

He put his arm around her shaking shoulder. "Don't worry. I'll protect you."

He stepped aside, slid the pack off his back, and brought out the axe. Legs spread a foot apart, knees slightly flexed, he glared ahead and turned in a complete circle, the snow in the clearing beaten flat by their activity. "Whoever you are, I have a weapon."

S ISTER AND BROTHER waited in silence, small vapor clouds emerging from their mouths with each breath.

"A weapon you say. What good a weapon is when your prey you cannot see?"

Shivers ran down Chloe's back, only these were not from melting snow. She backed up until her leg brushed against the tree on the sled. "P-Paul? Make it go away."

His eyes darted left and right. "There's no one there. Just a voice." He whirled around. "Show yourself ... if you dare." He raised the axe higher.

A brilliant light exploded in the air above them, then speckles of rainbow colors followed a tiny, winged figure. It moved so quickly Paul's fruitless swings with the axe slashed through the colors, which reappeared as soon as the axe left their path.

"Aha. See me, yes. Catch me, you cannot." The colors trailed the high-pitched voice of the figure that darted as fast as lightning.

"Paul. Stop. It's taunting you." Chloe moved over to her brother. She whispered in his ear, "Look at the pattern it made."

A small exclamation mark hung in the air, then fizzled out of sight, as did the tiny figure.

Paul lowered his arm, the axe dangling by his leg. "What is it?"

"I think the creature is a pixie. Maybe we shouldn't try to hurt it. It said it could help."

"Awe, pixies aren't real, Chloe. It's just kid talk. No one believes it." He looked up and around and shouted. "You hear that? We don't believe in pixies."

A hollow chuckle emerged from the air. The winged figure reappeared, out of reach but close enough to be heard and seen. Wings that beat faster than a hummingbird's kept it aflight. The sea green body wore forest green clothing with dark brown trim. Short black curls framed a face that seemed too small for the round black eyes that stared at the siblings.

"See me, you do. Believe in me, you do not? A simple-minded creature you are." The pixie darted about, more colors trailing its movements. Soon, the colors created a new outline.

Paul sputtered and dropped his axe. "I am not a donkey!"

Chloe turned away, covering her giggle with her mittened hand. Paul often made her think of a donkey when he got stubborn, which was at least once a week.

She got her giggles under control, then touched Paul's arm. "Don't pay attention to it. That's what it wants."

Paul scowled. "How come grown-ups say pixies aren't real?"

The pixie twirled a spiral in the air, sparkles trailing. "Grown-ups not believe, so cannot see. No fun for me. So, no play."

"How come we can see you, then?"

"See me, you can. Believe, you must."

Paul muttered more about not being a donkey and picked up the axe, slid it back in the pack which he secured to his back again. "All right. But how do we get out of here? The hill's too steep."

The pixie hung in the air before them. "Show you a way, I can. A path not so difficult. A path you can pull the sled."

Chloe stepped in front of Paul. "Why would you do that? Is this a trick?"

"There is a way, little person. No fun to me, if my game you do not play."

"You wanted us angry?" Chloe asked, hands on her hips.

"Yes. Fun. I like to play. You guessed my game, so now it must end." The pixie moved off to one side, farther into the woods. "The way is here. A path around the hill. A path for you to go. For cookies you share, I will take you there."

The pixie moved out of sight, leaving its trail of sparkles. Chloe looked at Paul and patted her pocket with the cookies. "These will get us home."

Paul nodded and shifted the pack. Then they followed the pixie deeper into the forest.

—— ⊸◦⊶ ——

AFTER THEY'D FOLLOWED the pixie for ten or fifteen minutes, Chloe turned to look behind them. "Paul," she whispered, "The sparkles behind us are gone. We won't be able to return if we get lost."

He leaned closer and whispered back, "Our footprints in the snow should be enough." He looked back and stopped. His face whitened, and his mouth dropped open. "They're ... they're gone."

"Paul? The sparkles ahead are gone, too." Tears streamed down Chloe's cheeks, and she did not bother to wipe them away.

Paul reached over and hugged his sister. "Don't worry," he whispered. "I'll get us home ... somehow."

Chloe shrugged off her brother's hug and stamped her foot. "I want to go home now. We'll get the tree tomorrow."

"But tomorrow is Christmas, Chloe. I wanted to surprise Mother ... make her smile. You know how sad she gets when Father is away."

"Why does he always go away?" Chloe scuffed her foot in the snow and wiped her nose. "It's not fair. Why can't he work in the same place every day like other fathers?"

Paul knelt on one knee in the snow and took her hands. "He's special. You're like him, all book smart and using big words. You'll understand ... some day."

She looked at him and smiled. "You think I'm smart like father?"

"Smarter than me, for certain. You'll grow up and be someone special, too. I know it." He grabbed the rope and began pulling the sled farther into the forest.

"How will you know which way to go?" Chloe followed, picking up the rope on the tail end of the tree and guiding it as Paul had asked earlier.

"The pixie said this way led around the hill. I think I know where we are."

"It's getting dark, and I smell snow coming. I don't want to stay all night in the woods."

"We won't, silly. If we keep going, we should be home soon. As long as the hill is on our right side, we're going the right way." He sped up, the deeper woods having little snow to slow them down.

The pixie came back, its brilliant sparkles trailing behind like the stars at night, only these were rainbow colored. It nodded and darted off again, returning every few steps Paul took, then darted off again, as if it could not contain its flight.

Chloe hurried to keep up and also to get home before dark. She was less afraid of the pixie now, but worried nonetheless. What if it decided there weren't enough cookies, or if it didn't like the flavor?

The next time the pixie reappeared, a set of white lights rushed up behind it. A larger pixie, the same color but wearing sky blue clothes with red trim, stopped beside the first. "Little people, said you. These are children. Nothing of the other world know you."

Pixie Green, as Chloe thought of it, said, "They are little compared to the others."

Pixie Blue cackled and whipped out a small wand. "Hup. Hup. Hup. Tree stand *Up*." The Christmas tree, sled still attached, rose upright. Paul dropped the rope before the sled pulled him up, too.

Pixie Green darted around the tree and in and out of its branches. "Hmm. This one will do." It looked at Paul and said, "A beautiful tree. Our clan will grant us favors for bringing it home."

Paul's eyes widened, and he stepped in front of the tree. "No. It is my tree. I cut it down for my home."

Chloe stepped forward. "We are bringing it home for our mother. She is sad and it will make her smile. Why do you need a tree when you live among so many?"

Pixie Blue looked at Pixie Green and chortled, its white sparkles taking on a darker hue. "Trick them, did you? Think they that you lead them to their home when the true path is over there?" It shot the wand out toward a small path barely wide enough for the loaded sled.

Pixie Green danced in the air, sparkles shooting off like fireworks on the Fourth of July. "Shush. Smart, you think you are. But give away my secret you did."

Paul and Chloe joined hands as the two pixies darted farther away and lowered their voices. As they argued, Pixie Blue kept its wand facing the two children.

———— ⚮ ————

C HLOE NUDGED PAUL. "Do you think Pixie Blue knows about the cookies?"

"What? Who? Oh, probably not. But how's that going to help?"

"If we keep them arguing, we could get away. I'll tell Pixie Blue about the cookies. If it gets mad, we'll know and can run."

"That's crazy, Chloe. And what about the tree?"

They looked behind them. The tree was back on the ground, resting on the sled. And it was facing the direction of the small path.

"OK. We'll take the tree, too." She gave her brother's arm a tug and said, "Start arguing with me."

"Why?" Paul scrunched his nose and rubbed it with his mitten.

"To get them back here. Then I'll tell the Blue one about the cookies and try to get them fighting more."

Paul nodded and stepped back from Chloe. "You said you'd help with the tree. Why do you want to leave it here now?"

"Mother doesn't need a tree. She needs us Home." Chloe stamped her foot and slipped, falling on her behind. She got up as the two pixies rushed over and hovered above.

"What say you, little one? The tree you do not want?"

Chloe pouted and said, "He made me help him when all I wanted was to go home."

Pixie Green hovered in front of Paul. "Bigger takes care of smaller. Is that not your way, too?"

Paul crossed his arms and straightened as tall as he could stand. "She's too stubborn. And always whining about being cold. She doesn't care about Mother being sad."

"That's not true, Paul. You're being mean." Chloe turned her back on her brother and faced Pixie Blue. "We were going to pay with cookies for your friend's help. Now you won't get any!"

"Cookies?" said Pixie Blue. "Cookies with sugar?"

"And cinnamon and raisins, too." Chloe patted her pocket. "Now you get nothing for trying to trick us."

Pixie Blue dashed over to Green. "Cookies! You said nothing about *cookies*."

Blue batted Green on the head with the wand. White sparkles burst from the wand, surrounding Green in a ball of light from which it could not escape. The more Green tried to free itself, the brighter and tighter the pattern of lights until it could not control its zig-zag flight. It tumbled in the air and away from Chloe and Paul.

Chloe pulled the bundle of cookie crumbs from her pocket and opened it. She threw a handful just past Pixie Green. "Here are your cookies, if you can get them from inside that bubble."

Pixie Blue squeed and darted after the crumbs, gathering as many as it could and stuffing them in its pockets. Pixie Green bounced along the ground, its arm reaching out for crumbs, but Blue was quicker. Chloe threw the rest of the crumbs farther into the woods, away from herself and Paul, and both pixies darted after them.

Chloe grabbed Paul's arm and pointed to the path home. He grabbed the sled's lead rope as Chloe picked up one on the trunk end, and they dashed off down the path.

The squeal of angry pixies echoed through the air. Chloe and Paul ran as fast as they could, the sled bouncing but mostly staying true to the narrow path between bushes and trees. It got stuck twice, but Chloe pushed against the chopped trunk and freed it faster than she thought possible. They had to make it out of the woods before the pixies caught up to them.

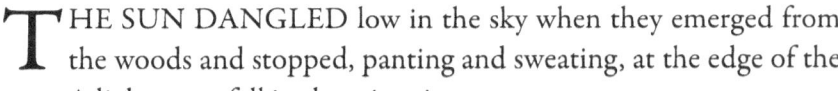

T HE SUN DANGLED low in the sky when they emerged from the woods and stopped, panting and sweating, at the edge of the trees. A light snow fell in the crisp air.

"We did it, Chloe. We're free." Paul hunched over, hands on his knees as he took deep breaths.

"Where are we?" Chloe brushed her hair off her face and tucked it under her hat. It snaked out and down her back as soon as she turned her head.

"This is Fritz's house. I've helped him pick vegetables from the garden." He pointed to a snow-covered tract off to their left. The snow ahead was deeper, where they'd have to create their own path through the yard.

"Mother must be worried, Paul. We have to let her know we're safe."

"Yes. Let's hide the tree behind the shed over there. We can come back for it tonight."

"If mother will let us out of her sight."

They forged a path through the deep snow, Paul dragging the sled behind them. They hid the tree, covering it with burlap Chloe retrieved from the shed. The sun was slipping below the tree line by the time they forced their way to the front of the house.

Mrs. Adams spotted them and rushed down the lane, lifting her long skirt as her boots splashed in the puddles this afternoon's sun had created in the tracks left by the horse carriages. She pulled them both into a tight hug. "Oh, my dear children. I had thought you lost in the woods."

She stepped back and brushed snow off Chloe's hat and pulled bits of snow from the girl's hair. "Just look at you two. Your mother has been frantic with worry." Her voice became stern. "Half the village is out looking for you. Hurry home. Hurry home."

She gently pushed them toward home, scolding as they walked, until they reached the front door. "Now go in, children, and let your mother know you are safe. I shall tell the others to call off the search." She bounded down the walkway, her voice booming, "The children are safe. They are home."

———— ◦◦◦ ————

C HLOE WOKE BEFORE dawn on Christmas morning and lay thinking. Was it real? Had it really happened? Her pants and boots lay on a heavy towel on the floor beside her bed. She reached out and felt the pants. Still damp. Yes. It had been all too real.

She slid out from beneath the heavy quilt, shivering as she put on a warm robe and slippers, and opened her door, looking both ways along the hallway before leaving her room. Holding her breath, she tiptoed past the stairs and glanced down at mother's closed bedroom door. With a sigh of relief, she hurried to Paul's bedroom at the end of the hall.

Not daring to knock lest she wake mother, Chloe slowly turned the knob to Paul's door, whispering his name as she cracked it open. "Paul. Are you awake?"

There was no answer, so she stepped into the room and closed the door behind her. His bed was empty. The window was open a tiny sliver. She rushed over and saw where he'd slid off the roof into the snow below and trudged off for the street. She sat on his bed, tears flowing. Why hadn't he wakened her?

She startled at the doorknob turning. Paul slipped into the room. "Don't cry, Chloe," he said, his voice low. "I saved the best for you." He sat beside her.

"What? You went and got the tree, didn't you?"

"Uh huh. After mother sent you to bed last night, Fritz came over. I told him where the tree was. We dragged it in this morning, but I haven't decorated it yet. I was waiting for you."

"Weren't you afraid you'd wake mother?"

"She took that drink last night that helps her sleep. But now I need your help to decorate the tree. Hurry. Get dressed and come downstairs."

She hugged her brother and rushed to her room as fast as she could without pounding her feet. Ten minutes later, she was downstairs where Paul handed her decorations and helped her reach the higher branches. When they were finished, he made cocoa and they sat by the tree.

Chloe picked up a leftover sparkling ornament. "I'm glad we escaped yesterday. I was scared."

"You didn't show it, much. And you outsmarted the pixies."

"Pixies? You don't believe those silly tales, do you?"

"Father!" Both siblings jumped up and rushed to their father's arms before he could close the front door.

"Now, what's all this about pixies?" He pushed the door shut with his foot and hugged the children.

"Pixies?" said mother, rubbing sleep from her eyes as she joined them. "Not those old stories again? There's no such thing."

Chloe gave Paul a knowing wink and said, "Of, no, Mother. Of course not. We don't believe in pixies."

Chains

I DIDN'T SET OUT TO be a hero. No one does. Burning building, child running into traffic, someone swipes the purse off a little old lady crossing the street—you react. Suddenly, you're a hero.

Today began like so many others. Up early. Coffee at the computer. Dress and leave for work. Make a mental note of the groceries to pick up on the way home. Traffic is light this early in the morning.

I report in to roll call, one of only two women on our small police force and listen to the cases night shift cleared. What's left open and important? Teen in a dark hoodie preying on senior citizens. Little thug waits until they're halfway across the street, then streaks across and knocks them over. Takes a purse, wallet, watch—whatever he can grab in a few seconds. Beats feet so fast the victims don't even realize they've been robbed.

Another domestic violence call last night at 133 Second Avenue, third floor. We've been there a lot, mostly at night. Husband's in jail now but he'll be out by mid-afternoon, wait and see. Wife never files charges. The report says the children, three and five years old, look like they haven't eaten in days. No money from him for food but there's always some for bail and booze. Child Protective Services will visit today. We'll go with CPS to make sure they're safe while doing their job.

The recital goes on, then we're free to hit the streets. I walk my beat alone, greeting store clerks and owners, checking IDs on youths in the basketball who look school-age but aren't, and basically being visible. My partner Roddy—Eddie Rodriguez—is home with his kids while his wife is in the hospital having baby number three. There was some problem with the birth, but he says mom and infant will be okay.

He lives in the neighborhood I've sworn to serve and protect, been encouraging me to move here. Maybe I will. He's taught me a lot since I joined the force a few years ago. Unlike some, he's never disparaged me for being a *woman in a man's world*. He never makes me feel I'm not up to the challenge of keeping his back covered in a situation—all one hundred and thirty pounds of me. Neither of us is suited to be chained to a desk, at least not now in our lives, but he's taught me to think ahead.

A beat cop has to be part cop, part social worker. Well, that's probably true of being a cop in general. But it seems more important when you're walking a neighborhood all day. As Roddy says, "Earn the respect of the people. Otherwise, you can't help them because they won't trust you."

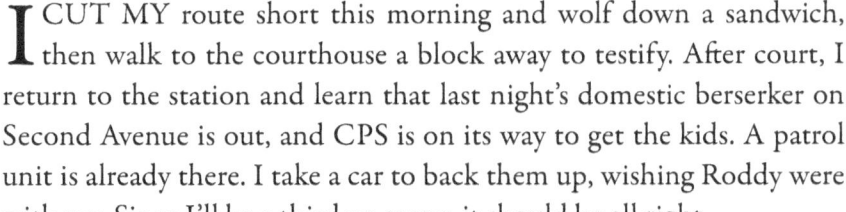

I CUT MY route short this morning and wolf down a sandwich, then walk to the courthouse a block away to testify. After court, I return to the station and learn that last night's domestic berserker on Second Avenue is out, and CPS is on its way to get the kids. A patrol unit is already there. I take a car to back them up, wishing Roddy were with me. Since I'll be a third on scene, it should be all right.

The trip to Second Avenue isn't long but I wonder the whole way—does the father ever go after the kids, hit them like he does the mother? Will CPS remove them from the home? What'll that do to the mother? My parents were poor, just barely scraping by on Dad's janitor's wages. They argued, but they didn't hit each other. Oh, I got spanked when I misbehaved, but a few swats on the behind doesn't leave behind bruises and broken bones like I've seen on this mother. We've tried to get her to leave—take the kids and go to a safe house where she can start over. Will she do it this time?

I ARRIVE AT the scene, one of several apartment buildings on the block. The rest is a mix of single-family homes and commercial buildings. Next to 133 is a three-story abandoned warehouse. Everything on the bottom floor was boarded up after evicting vandals who'd set the building on fire last year, but the broken upper windows remain untouched. Their second floor is about the height of the third floor at 133, so no one can get in from ground level.

Everything seems quiet as I park behind the first patrol car. Then shouting and breaking glass erupts. A chair lands in the narrow driveway between the apartment building and warehouse. Looking up, I see the mother jump from a third-floor window toward the warehouse. She makes it—almost—hanging by her fingers off the ledge of an open window.

She's gotta weigh over two hundred and fifty pounds. I pray she's got a strong grip. Seconds count and I'll never get the boards off the warehouse door in time. I run up the three flights in her building. The living room is first on my right and I smash out a window with a child-size chair, clearing the glass with my baton. Over the shouts and scuffling in the next room, I yell to the patrol unit that I'm on scene and helping the mother.

I take a running leap out the window, across the gap, and crash through a closed window, shielding my face with my arms. Most of the windowpanes were already cracked or broken, but I'm covered in glass as I tuck and roll. I stop at the edge of a gaping hole in the floor left from the fire. My radio slips from its holster and falls through—not good. I pull a large shard of glass from my thigh.

The mother's cries for help snap me back to the moment.

I rush to the other window and lock onto her wrists. "Hang on!" I begin pulling her up.

Her fright-filled eyes tell me she thinks she's going to die. The patrol unit across the gap is facing away from me as the husband struggles while being cuffed. Officer Donovan turns back and picks up an axe off the bed. No wonder she jumped.

Do they know where I am? My shout to them comes out as a weak croak. I'm out of breath from hauling the woman up so she can get her hands over the inside sill to hang on better. She's strong and athletic, despite her size, and uses her feet to gain leverage against the outside wall. Once her shoulders are past the windowsill, I yank her upper body inside, ignoring the creaks and groans of the floor beneath me. She's in far enough to make the rest of the way herself, which is good 'cause I'm on my butt on the floor.

As soon as she's safely inside, she turns on me, fear turned to anger. "You arrested Dickie last night. Now he's blaming me—why couldn't you leave us alone?"

Yada yada. Her tirade is familiar. Cops are good when they stop the victim from being hit, shot, knifed—whatever. Then we're evil because we arrest the abuser.

Roddy's words in my head calm me. "Abuse is a chain that tightens around the victim and drains all reason—leaving only fear, low self-esteem, and raw emotion."

She gets up from the floor and advances on me, the spittle coming faster than her words. "You took my babies—ruined my life. What do I have without them?"

Good, CPS had whisked the kids away before I'd arrived. I wouldn't want them to witness what's going on now. They've suffered enough, even if no one has hit them. Their scars will be emotional—the sudden intake of breath at the sound of a raised voice, the clenched stomach when they see a curled fist, that sudden drop in confidence when called upon by an adult and they don't have the right answer. Worse yet, they may grow up to become abusers—repeating the vicious emotional and physical pattern they learned from their father.

I stand and fend off her blows without retaliating, backing up each time she pushes me. We've made many calls to her apartment. Already, she's in the familiar pattern of pain and crisis, emotionally chained to the man who abuses her. I keep my voice low, soothing. "We're not your enemy. We're trying to keep you and the kids safe."

Nothing I say makes any difference. I let her get it out of her system while looking for a way out of here. Most of the floor is gone or so charred it won't hold much weight. She pushes me again and I step back, hearing too late the groan of the uneven floor. As it gives way beneath us, I grab her arm and pull her close to shield her from the long fall. I land on my back, on a mezzanine-type landing I didn't know was between the two floors. This, too, creaks and groans.

She rolls off me. I can breathe again. Pushing against the landing floor, I tempt fate and stand, motioning her to remain still. What's left of the floor is its own island, disconnected from everything except the support beam beneath us—and no way off. About twenty feet from where we landed, the exposed beam is cracked, almost split.

T HIS ISN'T MY day to die, I tell myself. I have too much life left to live. Roddy's face flashes across my mind. He's a good partner who's ignited my desire to go back to school, rise in the ranks of the department, and do more with my life outside of work. I want to become a detective and solve crimes, not die in a burned-out warehouse because some wife is too shell-shocked to realize we'd saved her and her kids' lives, not ruined them.

My radio is gone—no way to call for help. Do we have time to wait for a rescue? Did the patrol unit hear me say I was helping the mother? Can I get back to a window and call out for help? My bleeding leg throbs. The floor tilts and groans. Gotta get outta here.

The beams above us, at almost roof level, still hold chains and pulleys from the warehouse's days of hauling heavy items between floors. Can I use those to lower her, then me, to safety?

I turn to the mother. "Wait here. I'm gonna grab a chain and see if I can use it to lower you to the bottom."

She nods, no longer acting as if I'm the enemy. She looks more scared than anything. I crawl onto the thick beam on my hands and knees until I can reach a double strand of chain that runs through a pulley. Good, it has leeway in all directions. I crawl backwards, dragging the strands of heavy chain with me, palms and fingers splintered and bleeding from the rough beam. When I reach the landing, she helps me stand. I have no idea how safe that upper support beam is, so I pull with all my strength. It holds. We pull on it together. The beam and pulley hold against our combined weight, but not without some creaks and groans that make us both shudder.

We've said little since our fall, but she is compliant when I explain what I want her to do next. "I'll lower you to the bottom," I say as I slide my baton through one of the links. "Hold my baton tight. Use your feet to grip the chain." She grabs each end of the baton, her knuckles white with a hard grip.

"Good. Now wrap your leg around the chain, like this." I show her how. She looks at me askance but says, "Okay." Despite the quiver in her voice, she obeys.

"When I say ready, place your other foot on top of the first. It'll take some strain off your arms."

She hesitates and I add. "Look, you did great holding onto the window ledge. You can do this, too. I'll be holding this other strand to slow your descent."

Her face whitens more as she bites her lower lip. Can't she feel the floor tilting more with each passing second? We move to the edge of the opening, staying centered on the beam beneath us.

She takes a deep breath and hoists her full weight onto the chain, clamping one foot over the other with the chain between them. I hold the other strand and shift her position away from the beam and flooring.

It seemed like a good plan in my head. But as her weight shifts off the floor, the strand I'm holding rushes through my hands, burning through layers of skin. She's going too fast. She'll break her legs when she hits bottom. Ignoring my tears and painful, bloody hands, I grip tighter, wrap my legs onto the chain, and sag my rear end to let my weight help slow the chain's movement.

Splitting noises and more groans come from the beam above. Where's the patrol unit? They should have the husband in the car by now. This floor's falling apart. If I move off it, I'll go up but it should slow her down more.

Heavy banging noises from below distract me. I look down and see movement against the boarded-up doors. They'll be too late to catch her.

I yell down, "Jump off when you're near the bottom. Roll away, so the chain doesn't fall on you."

Passing seconds feel like eons. Can't wait. I swing out over the open area, all my weight on the chain to slow its momentum—just as the landing gives way. My one hundred and thirty pounds aren't enough to slow her descent for more than a few seconds. She continues down at a fast clip as I rush upward.

What's that? Is the upper beam cracking more? I daren't look. But I do. The beam gives way. The sudden break changes my direction and my rising body shifts to downward free fall.

"Jump," I yell.

I look down as the front door smashes open and the patrol unit pushes through, their upturned faces following her gaze as she points toward me. My body rushes toward the beam I leapt from oh so recently. I sigh with relief and pray she'll take this as a sign to move on with her life. I'm glad Roddy isn't here to see this.

I didn't set out to be a hero. No one does. It just happens. Today, it happened to me. Today, I died so someone else could live.

Tinsel

A CAR DOOR CLOSING woke me from my after-breakfast nap in the den. Crunch, crunch on the snow and the creaky squeak of the porch step. I grabbed a tennis ball and scrambled for the front door, all four feet slipping on the kitchen floor, and slammed into the fridge. *Oh, oh. Not supposed to run in the house. Not a great start to my day.*

I made it to the front door as Rebecca opened it. "Stay inside, girl."

Silly Rebecca. Mom taught me not to go out the front door without a person. I dropped the ball from my mouth and wagged as hard as I could. I love Rebecca. She smells so nice and lets me lick her face.

Mom came downstairs. "'Becca, I'm glad you're early. Here, let me take your bag. Your room's all ready." She picked up Rebecca's bag and was on her way upstairs before she finished speaking. Mom's like that. Go. Go. Go.

"I can do that, Mom." Rebecca started up the stairs after her.

"It's all right. I have to come up here anyway. Why don't you make some cocoa?" Mom disappeared around the corner at the top of the stairs as Rebecca came back down. I followed her into the kitchen and sat pretty for a treat. She put water on the stove and got out the mugs and cocoa. I'm learning more every day. Tea goes into cups, cocoa and coffee into mugs. Rebecca reached down and patted my head.

No treat? I slumped at her feet.

She took a small box from her purse and put it in a drawer, then looked at me and put her fingers to her lips, "It's a surprise for Mom."

The box was wrapped in fancy paper, like Mom was using yesterday. I'd gotten into the sticky stuff that holds the fancy paper on boxes, and Mom had to cut it off with scissors. I scratched where my fur was missing.

Rebecca reached back into her purse and pulled out a tennis ball. I took it just like Mom had taught me ... gentle, no teeth touching fingers ... and wagged.

Mom came in and they sat at the table. I took my ball to the den but could still hear them. Mom's voice is happy when she talks about me. Today was her sad voice, like when she talks about Roger. I never met him. Something about he was sick and then died.

Rebecca's voice wasn't her happy one, either. "Mom, I worry. It's your first Christmas without Dad. You're all alone in this house, and I'm so far away."

"Thank you, dear. But I'm fine. And Lucy's a delight. When I'm sad about Roger, she picks up my spirits."

"Well ... I read about the Christmas Present Burglars, thieves targeting neighborhoods with Christmas decorations. Yours are delightful, by the way. Are you sure you're safe?"

"We're fine, dear, really. Those break-ins are on south side, not here."

Their voices changed back to normal. Chickadees flew past the den window, back and forth between the fence and yard. Maybe I should go outside to protect them from the neighbor's sneaky cat.

Mom's voice floated through the air. "That Lucy. You can't believe the mess she made. I never thought her puppy legs could get up those steep attic stairs. Yet there she was, covered in tinsel. She ran off before I could grab her, and I found bits of tinsel everywhere for days."

They both laughed, so I must not be in trouble. My ball rolled under Mom's chair with the trapdoor. *Oh no!*

How does Mom make the bottom stick out? *Let's see ... she sits down and leans back.*

I jumped onto the chair and leaned against the back. Nothing. I threw my weight against it, again and again. It wouldn't budge.

"Lucy, what in the world are you doing?" Mom stood with her hands on her hips and a frown on her face.

Rebecca giggled. I threw myself against the seat back again, then jumped off and barked. She got on the floor and looked under the chair. I swiped her face with my tongue.

"Her ball's under here." Rebecca reached around the side of the chair, and the trapdoor opened. I grabbed my ball, and they followed me into the kitchen.

"Mother. Lucy is one smart dog."

"I don't get it."

"She must have seen you sit down and lean back in the chair to recline. When her ball got stuck, she tried to open it but didn't know about the lever."

"I hope she doesn't learn how to open the attic. Your father put a toe kick in the baseboard for me, not long before ... he got sick. He was so thoughtful and handy. It opens and closes the ceiling panel and the door at the top of the stairs. He put a switch up there, too, but I seldom used it. With Lucy climbing those stairs, though, I do now."

Rebecca said, "It was clever of him to replace those old stairs with the drop-down that tucks into the ceiling." She gave me a treat.

I gobbled it down and ran outside with my ball.

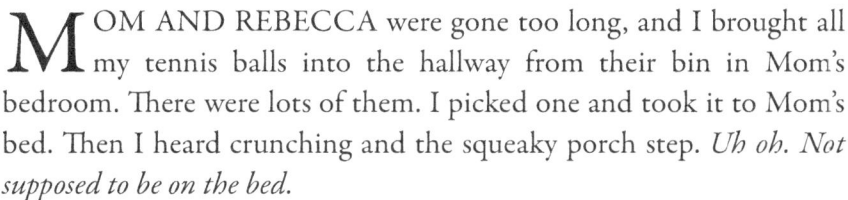

MOM AND REBECCA were gone too long, and I brought all my tennis balls into the hallway from their bin in Mom's bedroom. There were lots of them. I picked one and took it to Mom's bed. Then I heard crunching and the squeaky porch step. *Uh oh. Not supposed to be on the bed.*

I jumped off, yawned, and waited. Finally, the lock clicked.

Maybe Rebecca will play with me. I grabbed the ball and ran downstairs as the front door was opening. A really big man and a skinny man stepped in, whispering to each other. They shut the door real fast.

The big man yelled, "Get rid of that dog."

Yikes! I ran to the kitchen, out my little door, and hid behind a chair on the porch.

Where are you, Mom? Why are these strange men in your house when you aren't here? They don't sound nice, and I'm scared.

I couldn't hear them and poked my head through the little door. Upstairs. Mom wouldn't want these men in her room. She's par ...part ... part-ic-kular.

I sneaked up the stairs and stopped near the top 'cause their voices were close. I peeked around the corner. Skinny man was kicking the balls away from the attic stairs. They weren't down before. Big man went up and disappeared. Skinny man followed him.

Gotta see what they're doing. I'm good at being quiet, and they didn't hear me sneak up and watch from the top step. They opened Mom's trunks and boxes and threw things on the floor. Mom wouldn't like that. She always puts things away as soon as she is done with them. I ran toward them and barked, "Get out of here, you mean men."

One of them dropped a box on top of me. I wriggled my way out, but that shiny stuff was all over me. I ran down the stairs.

What a mess. Shiny stuff all over the stairs and hallway. Mom will be mad. I barked at them again.

Skinny man started down the stairs, so I ran and hid under Mom's bed. Skinny man stepped on a ball and fell near the bed and snarled. I growled back, then scampered out the other side, jumped on the bed, and leapt over him. He started to follow, but Big man yelled, "Never mind. It's just a puppy. Keep searching."

They made a lot of noise stomping around up there. I crept into the hallway and pushed the spot Mom always hits with her foot. The stairs slid up and hid the opening. They started yelling, and I ran downstairs to the kitchen.

I CREPT BACK upstairs and sat under the attic panel, waiting for Mom and Rebecca. I barked every time Skinny man and Big man made noise, and they've been real quiet since.

Mom's car pulled into the driveway. Crunch, crunch, squeak. I couldn't leave my spot.

"Lucy. I'm home. Where are you, girl?" Mom's voice.

I stayed where I was. She and Rebecca went to the kitchen.

"Rebecca, look at this. How did tinsel get down here? The attic was closed when we left."

"Mom, if she figured out how to open the recliner ... well, almost figured it out ... stands to reason she's learned to get into the attic." Rebecca called my name, then whistled.

I wanted to obey but stayed guarding the attic and growled. They went out to the car and came back two more times before closing the front door. *Why don't they come find me?*

"She's not on the porch. Not in the den, either." Rebecca's voice.

"She'd better not be sleeping on my bed. I know she does it when I'm gone."

Mom and Rebecca came up the stairs and turned the corner. Rebecca laughed, but Mom looked angry. "Lucy, how did you get into the tinsel again? Come here, right now."

I stayed where I was. Mom snapped her fingers. Rebecca crouched and called me. I wanted to go to her. It was so tempting. I looked up at the attic, at them, and up again.

Rebecca whispered, "Mom, it's like she's guarding the attic. Could someone be up there? Those were awfully big footprints by the walkway, and the front door opened almost before I finished turning the key. I didn't think anything of it at the time ...."

Mom gasped and put her hand over her mouth. She whispered in Rebecca's ear. Rebecca ran downstairs, and Mom came over to me. She crouched and stroked my back, picking pieces of the shiny stuff out of my fur like she wasn't mad anymore.

It felt like forever before Rebecca came back. She had a phone in her hand and whispered to Mom again. Was this a game?

I don't have time for games, Rebecca. There are bad men upstairs.

A few minutes later, the crunch, crunch, squeak came again. Rebecca ran downstairs and let someone in. Two men with guns came up the stairs and around the corner.

I backed up and growled. "Go away, mean men!"

Mom patted my head and said, "It's okay, Lucy. These are policemen, here to help. Let's get out of their way."

I followed her to the wall where she pointed to the special spot. The policemen told them to wait outside. Mom left the front door open, and we heard everything. One policeman shouted, "Whoever's up there, this is the police! This is the only way out. Drop any weapons down the opening and come down, one at a time."

More cars came with loud sounds and flashing lights. The neighbors came out and watched. Men and women dressed like the two policemen got out of the cars, went into the house, and brought the men out. They didn't look so mean anymore 'cause their arms were behind their backs. I barked at them, and Mom didn't even tell me to hush. I wanted to chase them, but Rebecca held my leash tight.

The two policemen who caught the robbers said everything was okay now. We went to the kitchen where I got a big treat while Mom and Rebecca talked to one policeman who wrote everything down. A policewoman came in and said they'd found the men's van around the corner, loaded with wrapped presents from houses in the neighborhood.

The other policeman patted me on the head and said, "Smart girl, Tinsel. You're the star, today. You helped us catch the Christmas Present Burglars."

I got bacon with dinner that night. *Yum!*

Kobyashi Maru

SUE WAS LATE, IF SHE was coming at all.

I was on my second walk around Red Rock Park at King's Beach in Lynn. The incoming tide, slate gray with white foam, rushed the seawall, splattering pedestrians, dogs, and bicyclists on the sidewalk thirty feet above. Storm coming.

To my left, high tide consumed the swimming beach. No swimmers yet; it's only April. I remained dry on the outer rim of the park's walkway. Rocks and boulders at the shoreline here and along the right side of the park form protective intertidal pools that buffer the waves. Two weeks ago, dozens of tiny dots on the water in the tide pools turned out to be baby ducks. Today, they were large enough to venture farther into the ocean, their mommas herding strays back into the group.

Where it once took twelve hundred steps to circle the park, I do it now in eight hundred, my cane giving me confidence to lengthen my stride and walk normally again. I'd never get the park down to the average of five hundred steps, not with my short legs and a back that popped if my stride was longer than it liked.

I didn't have it in me to do a third and rested on a bench. Come on, Sue. It's been a long day and I need to get home to the bathroom.

Dogs, some with owners and others without, passed the bench. I closed my eyes, inhaling the salty tang of the Atlantic. The sun's warmth was offset by a chill breeze.

FIVE MINUTES LATER, someone sat on the other end of the bench and said, "Susan's not coming." When I didn't answer, he repeated himself.

I opened my eyes and looked into a face with perfect features that drew—and held—my gaze. In nature and cosmetology, it's called Phi, the golden ratio. It was easy to understand why Sue had been smitten, if this was her boyfriend Matthew. Except now she wanted to extricate herself from him.

Tread carefully. If he's here ... "I don't know what you're talking about." My hand was in my jacket pocket, and I set my voice recorder on.

"Sure you do. What you don't know is that Suzie—"

Gah, how she hates being called that.

"isn't well. She has ... delusions. Thinks people are against her. She's done this before, so I'm not upset. I understand about her mental issues." He leaned toward me.

I started to rise, but he slid over and grabbed the leg of my cane. "Don't go yet. I want your assurance you'll leave Suzie alone."

"My cane is a mobility device. When you grab that, you grab me. Get it? Or should I call for a cop?"

He raised one arm in mock surrender, the smug smile never leaving his perfect face. "My bad. No harm meant." He hadn't let go.

I turned to a group of nearby walkers. "Can you help me? This man won't let me leave."

Two young men who could've been football players jogged over. "This guy bothering you?" One hooked his hand over the intruder's shoulder and squeezed.

Gritting his teeth, Matthew—I was certain now it was him—squirmed out from beneath the hand and ran away, shouting over his shoulder, "Remember what I said."

My two rescuers escorted me to my car, and I drove five blocks out of my way to make sure no one followed before heading for home only two blocks from the park. My 1950s garage had no electricity, so I got out in what was laughingly called the driveway—so short it was either park in the garage or on the street—and heaved the garage door open. *Ugh, that's getting harder to do every day.*

Nerves on edge, I ground the clutch when driving in. Normally I would exit through the same door, but it was too close to the street; I might be seen. I closed and locked the garage from the inside, checked my Ring app for intruders in the yard, and left through the side door closer to the house.

My fright must have put my bladder on hold because I was safe inside before heading for the bathroom. Rain splattered the windows, and the wind whipped tree branches into a frenzy—perfectly matching my jitters.

With a glass of wine to settle my nerves and a crackers and cheese plate for my stomach, I began my Internet search for Matthew Kingsley and his perfect face.

———— ⚬~⚬ ————

TWO DAYS LATER, the Dunkies' drive-thru line in Malden inched its way forward. Sue usually worked the pickup window. Sure enough, she was there today. As she scanned my payment app, I slipped her a burner flip phone with a note attached:

Leave on silent. Text me. Use phone for police or me only.

She slid the phone into her apron pocket and waved goodbye. How she could smile with that bruised cheek and wrist was testimony to what we can do when we must.

I worked in a haze all day, performing tasks that had become rote: assisted clients with applying for public benefits, checked the status of the previous day's filed tax returns—a special project I run—and a myriad of calls, follow-ups, and data entry logs. Meanwhile, my mind churned with ways to help Sue get out from Matthew's grip without losing her kids and her Section 8 housing.

She'd been my client for three years, and her story was both familiar and sad—and one I'd seen too often. Single mother of a young boy and girl ages ten and eight, two part-time jobs, and taking courses for a career she couldn't admit would be a dead end. Every step forward she'd taken had been followed by a setback. An abusive boyfriend completed her Kobayashi Maru—a no-win scenario aptly named in Star Trek* and roughly translated as "small wooden boat" that would not fare well in rough seas.

Her son outgrew his shoes and pants before they wore out. Luckily, her daughter could wear his hand-me-downs. Her refund, boosted with the child tax credit, would pay for school clothes and supplies and the son's after-school tutoring.

When this year's return had been rejected by the IRS because she had already filed under another person's return, I triple-checked before calling her. She'd come to my office that evening while a neighbor watched her children.

"Sue, did you know Matthew was claiming you and the children as his dependents?"

"No, Miss Loretta. He never said a word about it." She stifled a sob. "He never tells me what he's doing, but he's bad. He's going to get me kicked out of my housing, I know."

"If he's not supporting you, claiming you on his return is fraud. Is he living in your apartment? Is he on the lease?"

"No, not living with me. He stays a few nights, then he's gone for days. *I* pay my bills, not him. My Section 8 is only for me and my children. I don't want to be homeless, but he ..." she dabbed her eyes with a tissue, "... he has my spare key. I went to give it to the sitter one day and it was gone."

"You're certain he has it?"

"Yes." Her voice was now a whisper. "My neighbor, she told me he goes there after I leave for work. Cars come and go all day. Five minutes. No more."

"He's using your place for drug deals."

She nodded and wiped her nose with the tissue.

--- ❦ ---

SUE TEXTED ME after her Dunkies shift ended, thanking me for the phone, then added more in short bursts. She must have been watching over her shoulder for Matthew.

The day before, he'd told her not to see me again or contest his claiming her and the children as his dependents. I cursed, then wrote back to stay calm and not argue.

Matthew's brazenness alarmed me. He was protecting his comfy setup working out of her apartment. That made him dangerous. If he was using drugs, who knows what he might do?

It was ten-thirty before I could close the tax office. There was little traffic, and it took only a half hour to get to Lynn, taking the Revere route which sent me past Red Rock Park. Once home, I hurried out of my car to shut the garage door from the inside. The motion sensor light at that end cast an eerie glow in the small space. My spine tingled, even though I knew no one else was there. I searched the shelves, picked out a hammer and tire iron, and hid them beneath rags on the shelves along each side of my car. The wooden pole I had once used to brace my deck's sliding door would make a suitable weapon. I stood it next to the shelf at the front of the garage near the side door.

The Ring app showed an empty yard. I unlocked the side door, hurried to the house, and checked the metal brace securing the deck's sliding door. Next, I brought a tablet into the living room to keep one eye on the Ring's view of the front and back doors—even while watching television.

AFTER A WEEK of intense web searches in my spare time, I had pieced together Matthew's background. He had multiple accounts on all the social media platforms—including dating sites—and hopped from one to another with different names, girlfriends, and backgrounds. His face was the giveaway, with or without sunglasses, the mustache, then a beard, and now a goatee. I printed messages, images—everything connected to him—and organized it by date.

Every choice Sarah might made would end in disaster. We couldn't challenge Matthew's claim of Sue and the children as tax dependents without risking more bruises or worse. She couldn't ask the landlord for new door locks without a good reason, or he might simply make copies of his set. Matthew having a key to come and go was akin to his living there, violating her lease and Section 8 voucher. Of course, he'd lie if asked and say he was living there and she'd given him the key.

Being homeless with minor children was a bleak prospect. The state contracted with motels to house homeless parents and their minors. Unfortunately, some motels were the seedy rent-by-the-hour and don't-pay-attention-to-knife-fights-or-gunshots variety. If the only availability was in another part of the state, that meant disrupted schooling, changes in medical and other service providers, loss of sitter arrangements, and myriad other issues.

I couldn't call the drug tip hotline because if he were caught dealing drugs at her apartment, she would certainly lose her voucher and perhaps be charged with a drug offense and lose her children to state care.

I needed to set up Matthew for a drug bust away from Sue and her kids. First, though, Sue needed a crisis counselor who could whisk her to safety should things with Matthew worsen.

HUMAN SERVICES WORK is exhausting. The never-ending need against the limitations on what you can do is frustrating. Your reward is knowing you have helped someone whose need is greater than yours.

One advantage of my various jobs in human services over the years was a strong network of professionals in different roles. Sue's plight led me to call on Roy and Barry, two police officers I'd met at a previous job in a family housing development. They cared about the residents, knew everyone by their first name, and spent time with the kids in the development's after-school program. Their joy wasn't in drug busts and knocking heads; it was in seeing fear in young faces turn to relief when *these* officers knocked on a door in the middle of the night to break up a domestic dispute.

On Saturday, the three of us met for lunch at Victoria Station on Salem Wharf. It was too cool to eat outdoors, and we tucked into a quiet corner table where I had a view of the *Friendship*, a replica of a 1700s-era three-masted schooner that operates as a museum ship.

I told them what I knew for certain and believed were the risks for Sue, then handed over the printouts of Matthew's aliases, girlfriends, and changed appearance with each new identity.

Roy fingered the photos. "You've saved us some effort, Loretta. Got some good skills. But don't take risks. This guy will come after you, too."

"I know." I told them about my encounter at Red Rock Park. "I recorded it, but he said nothing useful or incriminating."

Barry rubbed his finger along his mustache and scowled. "Coward is what he is. What most of them are. What do you want us to do ... and not do?"

"Don't bust him at Sue's place. He'll blame her or me. But if he's followed from there to other places ... as long there isn't a straight line to Sue. Plus, you might get to his supplier."

Roy nodded. "There's a woman in the drug unit I'd trust with this. She ranks high enough to put the right team together. Meanwhile, we'll check these aliases, make sure we get Matthew's legal name right."

Barry gathered the files and placed his hand on my arm. "Does this guy know where you live?"

"I don't know. I've been taking a different route home every night since this started. But ... the park is close to my house."

"Be careful. Don't walk alone if you can avoid it ... at work or home."

I nodded, swallowing the rising lump in my throat.

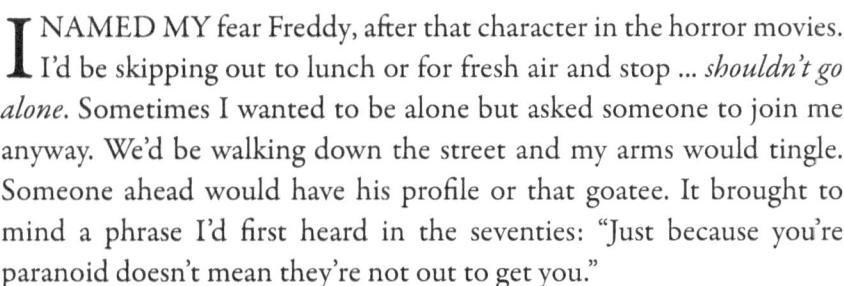

I NAMED MY fear Freddy, after that character in the horror movies. I'd be skipping out to lunch or for fresh air and stop ... *shouldn't go alone*. Sometimes I wanted to be alone but asked someone to join me anyway. We'd be walking down the street and my arms would tingle. Someone ahead would have his profile or that goatee. It brought to mind a phrase I'd first heard in the seventies: "Just because you're paranoid doesn't mean they're not out to get you."

I wonder if Sue feels like this?

The receptionist rang my desk; Roy wanted to see me. I went out to escort him to our work area, kept locked for everyone's safety. Some clients have *issues*: anger management, domestic violence, drug and alcohol abuse. Tempers can escalate over something as simple as a poorly chosen word.

Roy followed me to the conference room. I sat facing the hallway window. He sat opposite me and apologized for not calling first. "I got out of court early and thought I'd check on you before heading back to work. Have you heard from Sue?"

"No. Nothing in days. I'm worried. I wait for her to message me in case Matthew is near. He might hear the buzz of the vibrate setting."

"Good thinking. That phone is a lifeline. Someone like him would think nothing of going through her regular phone to read messages, see who calls."

"He did that already. That's why I gave her the burner. Have you learned anything new?"

"Barry and I think he's shacking with someone in the housing development. Like Sue, she may be an unwitting pawn. We followed him one night to the motel near the town line and passed it on to the drug team. The motel's a popular drug hangout."

We chatted for a few more minutes before he had to leave. On his way out, he turned back and said, "Make sure you're never in the building alone and someone helps you lock up at night."

"I've got that covered, but thanks for thinking about it. Terry, my buddy from the public access station, walks me to my car every night now. And I don't stay as late as I used to."

Guess my fear isn't paranoia after all.

I T HAD BEEN a month since my fright at Red Rock Park. I was closing the tax office when Sue texted me. Matthew had just left the apartment. He'd been staying nights with her and was moody, although she had avoided angering him. From work that day, she had used the burner phone to speak with the counselor I'd recommended.

Worry over her, and the distraction of stopping for milk and eggs for tomorrow's breakfast, must have made me careless. I pulled into the garage and turned off the headlights, then looked in the rearview mirror. No idea why, just did ... as a figure sidled in along the passenger side and ducked below the windows.

He must have been hiding on the other side of the stockade fence where it forms an L into the yard. The gate's been off for years.

My window was open, my ears on high alert. I still had my bone conduction headphones on and dialed 9-1-1 while popping the trunk, as if everything was normal. The rustle of cloth and a foot scraping against the cement floor gave away the intruder's location near my front bumper. The 9-1-1 operator asked if I needed assistance.

Three ... two ... one ... Wham! I thrust my door open and caught him as he was rising to stand. I bolted out of the car as fast as one can with a cane and slammed the garage door down before he got off the floor and reached it.

The lock clicked into place, but he could open it from the inside. It would take him a few minutes to find the latch, so I hustled around the corner into the yard, telling the operator I was being threatened by a burglar and gave her the address. Heart pounding, I pushed open the back door and slammed it shut behind me, leaning against it as I turned the deadbolt with trembling hands.

I SAT IN my recliner, despite Officer Franklin's refusal of a seat. "I don't know. Either I'd gotten careless and not noticed him following me, or he was waiting for me. What does it matter?"

"You didn't see him, so we can't be certain who it was."

Franklin's exasperation pissed me off. "Well, pick him up. If he's got a busted nose or something from my door whacking him, shouldn't that help?"

"He can say something else hit him." Franklin shifted from foot to foot. He apparently didn't want to be here any more than I wanted him here if he couldn't help.

"You found nothing in the garage that could be his?"

He spoke into his collar mic, listened, and turned to me. "My guy found a cap on the floor near your front driver's side. He's bringing it in."

Another crackle from the mic. "There's blood on the driver's door. Do you have any cuts or open wounds?"

"Nope. Not a one. Now we're getting somewhere. As for the cap, it's not mine and was not there before. Whoever belongs to that cap, that's your guy. His fingerprints should be all over the inside of the garage door."

My house sat on a corner, and another car with flashing lights joined the four or five police cars along both streets. The sidewalks were filling with curious neighbors. The officer who'd found the cap brought it in for me to identify. Another brought my briefcase and groceries in from the trunk and offered to put the perishables in the fridge.

"Thanks. That would be great." My frustration lowered when Roy and Barry, in plainclothes, stepped through the open front door. With them were two female officers, one from Lynn, the other Malden. The Lynn officer spoke to Franklin, who handed over his notes and stepped back.

Roy sat in the easy chair near me and raised his finger before I could speak. "Sue and her children are okay. A patrol car's watching her place."

"Oh, thank goodness. I've been so worried, and these officers," I pointed to Franklin and the others, "didn't seem to see the need to do anything."

Roy steepled his fingers and nodded. "Jurisdiction, Loretta." He pointed to the Lynn officer. "Francine has been collaborating with the Malden drug team and knows the whole story. She called me when she heard your address on the radio."

"Thanks."

"You should walk away from this," Francine said. "Sue's problem isn't yours."

"She came to me for help. She's my client. I have to see it through."

Roy shook his head. "You're asking for trouble."

CHIRPING BIRDS AND brilliant sunshine greeted me the next morning as if nothing had happened the night before. By the time everyone had cleared out last night, leaving a patrol car sitting in front of my house, I had been too tired to do more than fall into bed. Instead of nightmares, I had dreamed of the ducklings bobbing in the choppy ocean water, safe in their tidal pools with their parents hovering nearby.

Safety and security—that's all Sue wanted for her children.

I waved to the officer out front and brought coffee and milk to the back deck. The 7:00 a.m. shift wouldn't arrive for more than an hour since they'd have to check in at the station first. I rummaged for sugar and added a plate of muffins, then invited him to join me for an early breakfast.

He shook his head. "Can't see the front of the house from the deck."

I showed him my tablet. The Ring cameras satisfied him he could do his job. We chatted while I worked on my laptop.

Tax season was over; the only returns left were late filers, prior year returns, and amendments. I rescheduled those for daytime, early evening, or Saturdays. No more late-late nights for me until next January, but I still had nine o'clock closings on nights we held classes. They'd better find Matthew soon.

Roy had said the patrol car might need to respond to calls and emergencies. Ha! Lynn has tons of those every day. My skin itched as if ants crawled underneath. I'd faced angry clients and other tough situations, but nothing this intense.

THREE HOURS LATER, I packed my tablet to monitor the house from work and grabbed a flashlight on my way out the door, shining it into the dark corners of the garage before stepping inside. Barry had cleaned the blood and fingerprint dust from various surfaces inside. I shivered as I slid into the car and backed out, plastered a smile on my face, and waved to the day shift officer watching the house. In salute, he lifted the muffin I'd given him.

My offices were in a corner building on a hill. I parked on the main street in front of the tax office's street-level entrance and walked around the corner to the main agency. A police officer in the lobby nodded as I entered. I smiled back. When the elevator door closed, I leaned against the rear wall and released my breath, as if a loaded backpack had been lifted off my shoulders. *They're watching for Matthew even at my job.*

Roy called to say the prints in my garage matched Matthew, who had a record. The Lynn police had a warrant on him. My smile when greeting my next client was genuine, and the day flew.

Dusk was slipping into twilight when I closed the tax office. The deadbolt's satisfying click as I turned the key was followed by the rush of footsteps and a hand on my shoulder.

"Don't turn around." Matthew.

I froze, my raised hand still on the key in the lock.

"I've been watching you, saw the cop in the lobby today. Guess you thought you were smart."

My pounding heart and a rushing sound in my ears almost washed away his words. He jammed me closer to the door.

A shout from across the street. "Loretta, sorry I'm late."

Relief washed over me. Matthew shoved me in the back. My face hit the door as he ran off shouting, "I'm watching you."

Terry grasped my shoulders and spun me around. "You all right? Was that the guy ...?"

We went inside, where Terry got me a glass of water while I called and reported to Roy. "No. Don't come here. I'm going home. Now. Just find this guy and lock him up. I can positively ID him, but not tonight. Let me go home."

The patrol officer stationed at my home was standing in my driveway when I got there. He escorted me to the house and said he'd stay outside all night—no responding to other calls. *Thank you, Roy.*

———— ⟨∾⟩ ————

TWO DAYS LATER, police arrested Matthew at the motel after he'd left Lynn and headed toward Malden. Both departments were involved, interdepartmental cooperation at its best. Matthew, three other dealers, and their supplier were caught with drugs, cash, and weapons worth hundreds of thousands of dollars. Their outstanding warrants and prior arrests notwithstanding, firing guns at the police made their charges more serious.

Roy and Barry joined me and Sue for lunch—same table at Victoria Station. Her sitter was overjoyed at having work again and the knowledge that Matthew was out of the picture. Ron said he and the others had not been released on bail, Sue and I might not have to testify, and Matthew would definitely serve prison time even if he accepted the plea deal the DA had offered.

I'd never known how far I'd go to help a client until now, when I'd changed the rules and helped Sue overcome her Kobayashi Maru.

Acknowledgements

WHEN I BEGAN WRITING seriously, my first reader was my partner Pat Hill. An avid reader, she listened intently to each variation and offered constructive criticism, suggested word choices, and helped me improve my writing. With her support, I finished my first novel in six months. I wrote short stories, and she patiently worked through scenes with me to make them better. She lost her battle to cancer in 2019, but I still hear her voice in my ear, offering suggestions but, more importantly, encouragement.

My writing mentor, Edith Maxwell, suggested a critique group in Salem, MA. From Edith to Tricia Shepherd, the late Doug Hall, Margaret Press, Rae Franceouer, Elaine Ricci, and Sam Sherman, the Salem Writers Group helped me grow as a writer. Sisters in Crime offered workshops and networking that furthered my progress. After moving to Arizona in 2020, I got into write-ins hosted first by Anne Rainbow, then Kista Tucker, got into a critique partnership with Alicia Richardson, helped form a critique group with Erynn Crowley, Pat McGrath, Sarah Bolmarcich, and the late Faith Glick—later joined by Kista Tucker, and began my hosting my own write-ins for aspiring and experienced writers.

Painstaking progress on stories, a novel, and a trilogy put each chapter or story through a critique process that helped refine the end result. My sister Kathleen, with her keen eye for typos and word choice, adds her comments. Finally, Sarah Smith's *Tea Time with Sarah*, a small group of writers from Maine (Robin Orm Hansen), California (Zara Haimo), and Massachusetts (Robin Ray Hazard and Sarah) are another source of information and inspiration as well as listeners to tales in progress.

Writing may be a solitary process, but we aren't alone in the whole of it. For without these added eyes and ears, my words would not be in front of you.

About the Author

CLAIRE A MURRAY
Thinker | Planner | Doer | Author

Claire is a Phoenix, AZ, author of short stories and novels who misses her native New England but loves her new desert digs. She writes crime/mystery, fantasy, and sci-fi, and has been critiquing novels and short stories for fellow Sisters in Crime members for almost a dozen years. She hosts twice weekly write-ins to give aspiring and experienced writers a focused writing time and writes reviews for Kings River Life magazine—and occasionally for her blog.

Claire is the lead editor for the Desert Sleuths anthology *SoWest: Wrong Turn* (Sept. 2023). *Play the Hand You're Dealt* is a collection of her short stories, some previously published and others brand new. A member of Sisters in Crime, Mystery Writers of America, and the Short Mystery Fiction Society, Claire writes full-time, dabbles in painting, and lives on a steady diet of Zoominars for connection, inspiration, and sanity.

Claire is completing a suspense fantasy, has a trilogy in progress, and is writing the sequel to and revising her first novel before publishing it.

Learn more at https://cam-writes.com, *Where Character, Crime, and Mystery Collide* and https://facebook.com/clairemurraywrites.

Don't miss out!

Visit the website below and you can sign up to receive emails whenever Claire A Murray publishes a new book. There's no charge and no obligation.

https://books2read.com/r/B-A-KJONC-HZBCF

Connecting independent readers to independent writers.

www.ingramcontent.com/pod-product-compliance
Lightning Source LLC
Chambersburg PA
CBHW020957180626
46814CB00003B/1142